Die drei ???®

Die drei ???®

Soccer Mania

von Marco Sonnleitner

Aus dem Deutschen ins amerikanische Englisch übertragen von Andreas Zantop

Kosmos

Umschlagillustration von Silvia Christoph, Berlin
Umschlaggestaltung von Aiga Rasch, Leinfelden-Echterdingen

Bibliografische Information der Deutschen Bibliothek
Die deutsche Bibliothek verzeichnet diese Publikation in der Deutschen Nationalbibliografie; detaillierte bibliografische Daten sind im Internet unter http://dnb.ddb.de abrufbar.

ISBN-13: 978-3-440-10640-2
ISBN-10: 3-440-10640-3

Die deutsche Originalausgabe erschien unter dem Titel
“Die drei ??? – Fußballfieber”
bei Franckh-Kosmos Verlags-GmbH & Co. KG.
(ISBN-13: 978-3-440-10207-7)

Übersetzung: Andreas Zantop
Bearbeitung: Ursula Tzavaras, Vivien Arnold
Redaktion: Julia Röhlig, Martina Zierold
Produktion: DOPPELPUNKT Auch & Grätzbach GbR, Stuttgart
Printed in the Czech Republik / Imprimé en République tchèque

Die drei ???®
Soccer Mania

Shaw against Jonas

"The ball flies diagonally across half the field and lands at … Shaw! Yes! Shaw's got the ball! Just wonderful how he stopped it with the chest while running! With the right foot, he now drives the ball towards the **penalty area**! But now! An opp…"
"Peter! That's close enough!"
"… An **opponent** blocks his way! It's – oh no – El Torbellino, the Whirlwind! Will Shaw be able to get around him? Will he make it? Shaw pretends a motion to the left, then, with one, two **deke moves**, and – yes! He gets around El Torbellino! He really fooled him this time! Fantastic! Simply **ingenious**, this trick, simply ingenious, this Shaw guy!"
"Peter! If you drive the ball too hard again …"
"Now all he has to do is to get around the goalkeeper! But Jonas is a real heavyweight; it's not so easy to find a gap!"
Bob laughed, **slapped his thighs** and applauded enthusiastically. "Great, this commentator!"
Justus looked at him furiously, but then he concentrated on the old leather ball again which Peter chased across the junkyard **without remorse**. '**What the heck** am I doing here?' Justus asked himself – not for the first time, by the way.
"Shaw puts the ball on his strong left foot. For a second, he looks up, checks which corner to choose, shoots and …"

---

penalty area – Strafraum; **opponent** – Gegner;
deke move – Übersteiger; **ingenious** – genial;
to slap one's thighs – sich auf die Schenkel klopfen;
without remorse – gnadenlos;
what the heck … – was zum Teufel/Kuckuck …

The ball came flying towards Justus with incredible speed. The First Detective had just enough time to pull in his head. With a low whistle, the leather ball whizzed by – into the goal.
"Oh man, Just!" Peter complained. "You're not supposed to duck down every time the ball comes your way!" He stood, arms **akimbo**, looking at his friend **reproachfully**. "You're supposed to dive for the ball and catch it!"
Justus straightened up and tapped his forehead. "Are you kidding? I'm not **suicidal**! I told you not to hit the ball so hard."
"But it wasn't that hard at all!" Peter called.
Justus smiled at him ironically. "Well then, why don't you ask Bob if he would like to be goalie and face some hard hits. I, for my part, have served as target long enough. The heavyweight," Justus **exaggerated** the pronunciation of the word, "officially ends his practice now."
"Just! Please!" Peter looked at his friend **imploringly**. "Bob will do the dribble training with me. But I do need to practice some more goal shots. You know, in three days there will be …"
"… the first final of the California School Soccer Championships," Justus and Bob said, almost in chorus. They looked at each other **baffled** and then started laughing loudly.
No wonder they thought and said the same thing at that moment. For days, Peter hadn't talked about anything other than this soccer game. There was hardly any other topic for him since he had reached the final with his team.
However, Peter didn't just talk about it, but practiced day and night: dribbling, running, shots on goal, no matter whether

---

akimbo – in die Seite gestemmt; **reproachfully** – vorwurfsvoll;
suicidal – lebensmüde, selbstmörderisch; **to exaggerate** – übertreiben;
imploringly – inständig, flehentlich; **baffled** – verdutzt, verblüfft

on the soccer field, at the bus stop or in school, and no matter whether with a can, an empty milk carton or with a ball. Everything was kicked around, every traffic sign was an opponent to get by, every gap or hole served as goal. And as always, Peter acted as his own sports commentator.
This afternoon he had held his practice at the junkyard of the Jonas family. Mathilda and Titus Jonas, Justus' aunt and uncle, ran a shop for second hand articles. Actually, Mathilda had asked the three boys to sort out the contents of some boxes that Uncle Jonas had brought along from the **clearance** of a household. But in one of these boxes Peter had found an old leather ball, and right away, the fever gripped him again. He actually begged Justus and Bob to practice with him a little. Just a little bit – they could still sort out those boxes afterwards. And because Justus and Bob knew that Peter would **nag** and urge them until they finally would, they **eventually** agreed.
But it did cost Justus quite some effort. The First Detective wasn't particularly good at sports – due to a few pounds too many. In addition, he didn't really know much about playing soccer. In California, basketball, football or baseball were far more popular. Therefore, he could only guess vaguely what would come his way. But for Peter's sake, he finally gave in and positioned himself between two stacks of old car tires, serving as goal posts.
But he would **regret** having done so very soon. What Peter claimed to be 'practice' turned into a real suicide commando. Peter didn't practice moderate goal shots, he shot canonballs at

---

clearance – (hier:) Auflösung; **to nag** – keine Ruhe geben, nörgeln; **eventually** – schließlich, letztendlich; **to regret** – bedauern

him! Very soon, Justus felt like a **clay pigeon**, and instead of going for the ball he **dodged** it as best as he could.
"Justus! Please!" Peter gave it one last try. "Our coach Bridges said that everybody on the team has to give his very best. Otherwise, El Torbellino will demolish us! He'll finish us!"
A few days ago, Peter's **pleasant anticipation** of the game turned into serious **concern** over it – namely when he found out who they had to play against in the final. However, it wasn't the opposing team as such that caused him **discomfort**, but one single player: El Torbellino, the Whirlwind! Peter didn't know the guy, he had never seen him before. But it was said that he was an exceptionally talented player. Obviously, he had even attracted the attention of talent scouts from European top clubs already. And that's saying something: these clubs usually sent their agents to South America or Africa – but not to the USA.
But then again Justus **was fed up**, with or without El Torbellino. "Peter, I'm sorry, but I'd really like to live a few more years. Besides – if we don't get back to our boxes soon, I fear for *your* lives as well." The First Detective pointed towards the house. Peter and Bob understood. Aunt Mathilda would soon come around to check up on things, and she would not be particularly amused to find the boys **idle**, kicking the ball around when they should be working.
Looking at the house, they noticed a boy who stood in the gateway of the junkyard. He was about their age, at least as tall

---

clay pigeon – Tontaube; **to dodge** – ausweichen;
pleasant anticipation – Vorfreude; **concern** – Sorge, Besorgnis;
discomfort – (hier:) Unbehagen; **to be fed up** – genug haben, die Nase voll haben; **to be idle** – untätig sein

and strong as Peter, with a very dark skin tone, and his deep black hair was shimmering bluish in the hot afternoon sun. His **facial features** seemed to indicate that he was a Latino – either of South or Central American, perhaps Mexican **descent**. Die drei ??? recognized at once that he seemed somehow uncertain, the way he stood around at the gate. He looked at them almost **furtively**, wringing his hands all the time – but didn't **dare**, for some unknown reason, to enter the junkyard.
"I wonder if he wants something from us?" Peter asked and looked at his friends.
"Perhaps a customer?" Bob wondered and pulled up his eyebrows.
"I don't think so," Justus replied, "but we'll find out in a second." He waved at the boy and, when he waved back shyly, Justus called out loud: "Can we help you in any way?"
"Uh … well … yes," the boy answered with a low voice, then raising his voice a little more: "Yes, I … I think so, yes. Are you the three detectives?"
For a moment, Justus, Peter und Bob looked at each other in surprise. Indeed, the boy had come to see them. Then Justus answered: "Yes, that's us. Wait! We're coming."
Together they walked down to the gate. The boy stretched his hand out towards Justus: "Hello," he said, smiling shyly to the three boys. "I'm Emiliano. Emiliano de la Cruz."
"Hello, and I'm Justus."
"Peter."
"Bob."

---

facial features – Gesichtszüge; **descent** – Abstammung; **furtively** – verstohlen, heimlich; **to dare (to) do sth.** – (es) wagen etw. zu tun, sich trauen etw. zu tun

Emiliano shook hands with the other two detectives as well. Then he looked down to the ground for a moment, took a deep breath and finally said: "I came to see you because I heard that, perhaps, you could help me. Uh, I mean that you could help us, for that matter. Or my grandparents, that is …"
Quite obviously, the boy was a little confused, or somehow uncertain – or both. So Justus decided to ask him to come inside, first of all. Chances were that the boy would eventually calm down a little.
"Emiliano, let's go over to our **headquarters**," Justus suggested and pointed towards the old trailer to the left of them in the back part of the junkyard. "There you can tell us in detail what's on your mind."
Emiliano nodded **bashfully**, and the four of them walked across the yard to the detectives' headquarters.
The headquarters were the center of the little detective agency founded by die drei ??? a few years ago. Over time, they had gradually expanded and upgraded the old camping trailer, so that, meanwhile, everything needed for such a business was on board: a telephone with an answering machine, a computer with Internet access, a small **Xerox-machine**, a fax machine – and even a darkroom with a lab for minor **forensic** investigations. There wasn't much space left in the trailer, however, and the old chair Emiliano was supposed to take a seat in had to be cleared of some stuff by Peter first.
"OK," Justus said, once all of them had found a place to sit, "now tell us. What is it that we should help you with?"

---

headquarters (pl.) – Zentrale, Hauptquartier; **bashfully** – scheu, verschämt; **Xerox-machine** – Fotokopierer;
forensic – (hier:) kriminaltechnisch

Emiliano, sitting on the edge of the chair, still **hesitated** for a moment. Then he started talking, but he didn't look at die drei ??? while doing so. "My little brother Pedro and I, we live with our grandparents in San Fernando. My parents died a few years ago in a car accident in Peru. Our grandparents, Esperanza and Pancho, are loving and **endearing** people, but they are also quite old already. Sometimes I can't really follow what they say and do. But that's not the problem right now. Because, even though I don't see the things that recently happened at our place the way they do, it is still very … strange."
Die drei ??? didn't say anything at this point. They wanted to hear the whole story from Emiliano. Puzzles or **inconsistencies** could be sorted out later.
Emiliano continued: "I've thought a lot about what could be going on, but I just can't come up with an explanation. I don't know who could be doing something like this and why. I myself probably wouldn't care about it because I don't take the whole thing so seriously. But my grandparents suffer from it more and more, and that's why I …" The boy looked up at die drei ??? now. "That's why I came here to see you. I was told you **are familiar with** stuff like this, and that, perhaps, you could help us. And I was also told," Emiliano hesitated for another short moment, "that you don't take any money. You have to know that we don't have much money. I just don't know how to pay you …"
"Don't worry about that," Justus interrupted him and waved it aside, **putting** Emiliano **at rest**. "Indeed, we don't take any

---

to hesitate – zögern, zaudern, **endearing** – liebenswert; **inconsistency** – Ungereimtheit; **to be familiar with sth.** – mit etwas vertraut sein; **to put so. at rest** – jmd. beruhigen

money for our investigations – in fact, we never did. But now tell me," Justus smiled at Emiliano **encouragingly**, "what happened at your place, after all? What is it that your grandparents are worrying so much about?"
Bob and Peter nodded. They also wanted to know now what the deal was.
Emiliano bit his lips. "Some strange things happened. Nothing really bad, as I first thought. But my grandparents were immediately convinced that ... " Emiliano paused abruptly, shook his head and said: "You know, it's crazy. My grandparents are very **superstitious**, that's one thing I know. And this time I have to admit that, after my **inquiries**, they seem to be right with their **superstition**. Well, I don't really mean they are right. But strangely enough, everything that's happening can actually be explained the way they do. Everything fits perfectly somehow."
"But what is it?" Peter asked, slightly impatient by now. "What's going on?"
"All these things that happened in the last few days and weeks at our place," Emiliano answered slowly, "are, according to my grandparents ... **harbingers** of death! They actually believe that someone in our family will die soon!"

---

encouragingly – ermutigend; **superstitious** – abergläubisch; **superstition** – Aberglaube; **inquiry** – Nachforschung, Erkundigung; **harbinger** – Vorbote, Zeichen, Omen

A new case for die drei ???

"This must be it." From the backseat, Bob leaned forward between his two friends and pointed at a street sign. "Oakwood Street. Emiliano said we should drive all the way to the end of the street; their house would be down there on the left side."
Peter signalled a turn and steered his MG into the narrow side street. "I'm really curious now," he said, looking expectantly at Justus who was sitting beside him in the front passenger's seat. "I can't really **wrap my mind around** this 'harbinger of death' thing ... Particularly when I think of what Emiliano mentioned as harbingers: lilies, a red knife, owls hooting, clocks showing the wrong time, hmm." Peter looked doubtful.
Yesterday, Emiliano had told them the main facts about what had happened at his home recently, and what it was that got his grandparents so terrified. But the whole thing sounded so strange and **obscure** that the three detectives couldn't make any sense of it. Thus, they had asked Emiliano if they could take a look at all this on his grandparents' **premises**, and the boy immediately invited them.
Looking back on it, die drei ??? **assumed** that this was exactly what he wanted to ask them all along – if he hadn't been so shy and confused. Afterwards, Emiliano described to them in detail where he was living and, visibly **relieved**, said goodbye to Justus, Peter and Bob.

---

to wrap one's mind around sth. – etw. verstehen, sich vorstellen; **obscure** – undurchsichtig, verworren; **premises** (pl.) – Gelände, Anwesen; **to assume** – annehmen; **relieved** – erleichtert

The next morning the Second Detective picked up his friends in his MG, and together they drove to San Fernando. Actually, they had originally planned to drive one day later. Today was Sunday, and they thought that the de la Cruz family would like to be on their own. But Emiliano nevertheless suggested that they should stop by today.
The place was northwest of Los Angeles, about a 45 minute drive from Rocky Beach, and turned out to be a number of rather poor looking houses and a few small farms. Just a single broad main street led through San Fernando, and about a dozen side streets branched off to either side. The village was surrounded by a totally flat, **sparse** steppe with countless cactuses reaching into the **hazy** sky like oversized fingers. To the west, a bald rocky mountain ridge with a few **jagged** slopes was rising behind the village limits, **merging** into the foothills of the Santa Monica Mountains.
"Well, we'll see in a minute what this is all about," Justus picked up Peter's thoughts. "Maybe it's all **sheer coincidence** after all, or someone is playing dirty tricks. But it's also important to get sense for these grandparents. We have to find out why these incidents **agonize** them to such a degree."
"You mean," Peter grinned, "the couple might turn out to be a little … odd or **queer** … due to their old age?"
Justus **shrugged**. "Or have been all the time. Superstition is not something to be found only in older people. But who knows, perhaps there's something else or even more behind this."

---

sparse – karg, spärlich; **hazy** – dunstig; **jagged** – schroff, zerklüftet;
to merge – übergehen in; **sheer coincidence** – purer Zufall;
to agonize – quälen, martern; **queer** – seltsam, komisch;
to shrug – mit den Schultern, Achseln zucken

"What do you mean, more?" Bob asked. "What other reason could there be, in your view, why they are so concerned by these incidents?"
Justus pointed through the windshield to a house. "Let's find out. We are here. This should be the de la Cruz's house."
Oakwood Street ended a few feet further down. To the left, a small, not particularly luxurious house appeared behind a big hedge belonging to the neighboring premises. It was a two-story building with a **roofed patio** on the front, painted a color somewhere between yellow and brown. An aged wooden fence ran parallel to the street. Behind it, some chickens were picking around in the dust. To the right of the building, a few trees were growing, and to the left, a gray pickup truck stood under a poorly constructed **shed**. In the background there were a few flowerbeds, and they could also see parts of a **tool shed**. Behind that, the steppe began.
Peter parked his MG right next to the front gate. They were just about to enter the premises when the door opened and Emiliano came out.
"Hello! Good to see you!" he called out and came towards them. Behind him, a small, **chubby-faced** boy with **tousled** black hair came out through the door to meet die drei ??? as well. He had bare feet, and **remnants** of his breakfast were visible around his mouth.
"How was your trip? Did you find our place right away?" Emiliano asked, shaking their hands one after the other.
"No problem," Peter replied. "Your description was very precise."

---

roofed patio – überdachte Terrasse; **(tool) shed** – (Geräte-)Schuppen, Bretterverschlag; **chubby-faced** – pausbäckig; **tousled** – verstrubbelt, zerzaust; **remnant** – Überrest

"Are those the detectives?" the small boy whispered to Emiliano, looking at die drei ??? almost with **reverence**.
"Justus, Peter, Bob! This is Pedro, my brother. Pedro, these are the famous drei ???," Emiliano introduced them.
The three detectives said hello to Pedro, but the boy was unable to say anything at all and just **gaped** at them. Obviously, he was meeting real detectives face to face for the first time in his life – and he was deeply impressed.
"Come on in!" Emiliano pointed towards the door, and Pedro ran ahead. "I'd like to introduce you to my grandpa. However," Emiliano paused, looking a little embarrassed, "I have to warn you in advance. Grandpa Pancho is a little, well … strange. And he wasn't really thrilled when I told him that you'll be coming. He thinks that will make things even worse. But we do need your help, and grandpa will understand that sooner or later. You'll have to believe me, he is a really lovely person. Just don't take everything he says too serious. Basically, he doesn't really mean it the way he says it."
'Well great!' Peter thought to himself. 'That really helps.' He looked at Bob skeptically, and the third detective didn't give the impression that he just couldn't wait to meet Emiliano's grandpa. Only Justus seemed to be relatively unaffected, and with resolute steps he followed the boys into the house.
"Grandpa!" Emiliano **yelled** while he escorted die drei ??? through a small dark hallway. He opened a curtain made from knotted sisal with wooden **beads** woven into it, and together they entered the living room. It wasn't particularly **spacious** but flooded with light, with a welcoming interior and nicely clean.

---

reverence – Ehrfurcht, Verehrung; **to gape** – (mit offenem Mund) anstarren; **to yell** – rufen; **bead** – Perle; **spacious** – geräumig

"Grandpa! These are the boys that …"
"Don't call me grandpa all the time!" The grumbling voice belonged to an old man sitting at a table reading the newspaper. "That's *Abuelito*. Or just *Pancho*. But not grandpa!" The man turned around, looking angrily at the newly arrived boys. His sunburned face was covered with countless **wrinkles**, making it almost look like a piece of tree bark. He had lots of white hair which looked quite messed up, his clothes were simple yet colorful, and a curved wooden pipe was sticking in the left corner of his mouth.
"Abuelito," Emiliano started again, "these are Justus, Peter and Bob. You know. The three boys that …"
"Of course I know. After all, you told me, and I am not **senile** yet. Those are the three boys that think they know more about the things going on here than your old abuelito. Pshaw!" He sucked on his pipe **vigorously**, examining die drei ??? with visible **contempt**.
"Abuelito, please, you told me that you would at least listen to what the three boys think about all this."
"Well, what could they think? Why should they know what's going on here? Hmm? Three gringos!"
"But I …"
"Señor de la Cruz," Justus now started to speak. "First of all, I'd like to tell you that we are far from pretending to know anything better than you do, particularly because we don't have any detailed information on what really happened here. Your grandson only asked us to take a look at the mysterious events going on here for some time now and which he thinks

---

wrinkle – Falte, Runzel; **senile** – senil, verkalkt; **vigorously** – kräftig, energisch; **contempt** – Geringschätzung, Verachtung

are **disturbing** you and your wife. And as we do have some experience in dealing with **seemingly inexplicable** phenomena, we did what he requested and came to you today. But of course, we will only offer you our services if you really want them. That goes without saying. However, I'd like to point out that we've been working on similar cases like this one, often with surprising success." Justus smiled **obligingly**, pulled out a small metal box from his pocket and opened it. Then he took one of their self-made business cards which each of die drei ??? always carried with them, and held it out towards the old man. "May I kindly hand you our business card?"

Peter and Bob tried not to laugh. Right from the beginning of Justus's speech they knew what he had in mind. The First Detective wanted to use his acting talent, shown often before, to impress the old man. Pancho should not consider them as ordinary and curious teenagers, but rather see them as **reputable** detectives dealing with his concerns in a calm and professional manner.

And indeed: Pancho was impressed. For a second, he even forgot to suck on his pipe after Justus had stopped speaking. Without a word, he looked at the First Detective and **absent-mindedly** took his card. A few seconds later he seemed **to recover**, now carefully **scrutinizing** the business card of die drei ???.

---

to disturb – beunruhigen;
seemingly inexplicable – scheinbar unerklärlich;
obligingly – verbindlich, zuvorkommend;
reputable – seriös, angesehen;
absent-mindedly – geistesabwesend;
to recover – (hier:) sich fangen; **to scrutinize** – prüfen, untersuchen

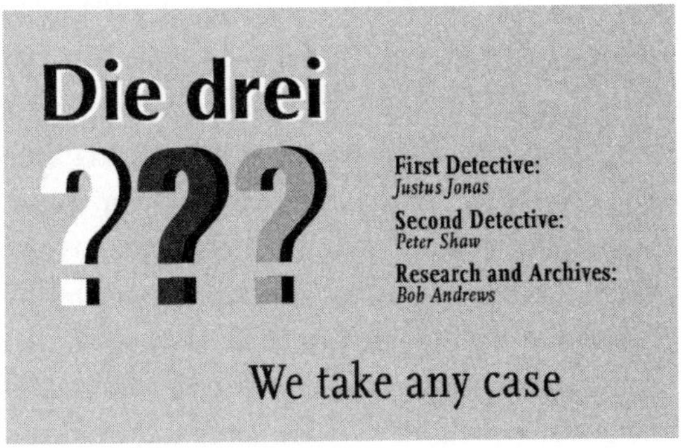

"Die drei ???," Pancho read slowly. "We take on every case. Hmm. Why are there three question marks on the card? What's that supposed to mean?" The old man looked at Justus with an unfriendly expression. The eloquent speech of the First Detective had not silenced him long.

"The question marks," the first Detective replied in a friendly manner, smiling obligingly, "are a symbol for all those unsolved puzzles and **secrets yet to be disclosed**."

"Is that so," Pancho **snarled**, "secrets!" He returned the card to Justus, adding almost **sullenly**: "But there are no secrets to be disclosed around here. The things happening around here are not inexplicable or mysterious at all. They are quite clear – if you know how to interpret them."

Justus was **moaning** inwardly. Indeed, the old man was a hard nut to crack.

"All the things happening here are certain signs," Pancho continued, looking sharply at Justus with his dark eyes. "Signs that

---

to disclose a secret – ein Geheimnis lüften; **to snarl** – knurren; **sullenly** – trotzig, mürrisch; **to moan** – stöhnen

want to point out certain things to us. And we don't need anybody to explain to us what those things could be. We already know what they are." Emiliano's grandfather had raised his forefinger in a threatening way while talking to the three detectives. He was just about to turn away from them when he thought of something else. "And all this **concerns** only us," he said in an excited tone of voice. "It concerns our family. And so we have to make up our minds about what to do. If something can be done at all, that is. Perhaps we can still change our **fate** for the better. But if not, if we can't change our **destiny**, it might be just as well. Then we'll …"

Suddenly the old man fell silent. Emiliano and Pedro **grew stiff** as well, and die drei ??? turned around almost at the same time. From outside they could hear a screaming cry of fear!

---

to concern – betreffen; **fate** – Schicksal; **destiny** – Bestimmung; **grew stiff / to grow stiff** – erstarrte / erstarren

An army of burying beetles

"Grandma!" Emiliano's voice sounded **hoarse**. "Grandma!"
"Esperanza!" Pancho de la Cruz **staggered** and had to hold on to a chair.
"It came from that direction!" Peter yelled. "From the garden!"
"Quick!" Bob ran out of the room. "Come along!"
Justus and Peter followed him at once. For a few seconds, Emiliano was stiff and motionless. Then he followed the three detectives as well.
"Around the house!" Peter was **gasping** when they stood on the veranda. "We have to run around the house! I'm sure it came from there."
"Stop! Look!" Justus held on to Peter's sleeve and pointed towards the street. Just that moment, the shadow of a car disappeared behind the blackcurrant bushes. One second later, they could hear the sound of a car starting up. "A car is taking off! Peter, go after it!"
"Okay! Right away!" The Second Detective felt for his car keys and jumped down the stairs of the veranda.
Justus and Bob ran the few feet towards the corner of the house and looked around it. They discovered the old lady at once. Just a few feet away, she sat on the ground in front of the small tool shed in the corner of the garden. She was surrounded by pieces of a broken flower pot, piles of **soil** and blossom leaves. She was breathing heavily, staring at the ground with a confused look.

---

burying beetle – Aaskäfer; **hoarse** – heiser; **to stagger** – taumeln, schwanken; **to gasp** – keuchen, schnaufen; **soil** – Erde

"Grandma!" Emiliano yelled behind them in **desperation**. "Grandma, what happened to you?"
Within a few seconds, the three boys were next to Emiliano's grandmother.
"Señora de la Cruz? Are you okay?" Bob asked anxiously.
"Grandma! Abuelita!" Emiliano kneeled in front of his grandmother, putting one hand on her cheek. "What is it? What's the matter?"
Justus and Bob stood in front of the old lady and looked at her worriedly. At first glance, it didn't seem as if she had fallen down. She didn't have any visible injuries either. To the boys it seemed as if – for whatever reason – she had simply dropped down next to one of the flower beds. And now she was just sitting there in her green garden **apron**. She was **panting**, had a fixed stare in her eyes and was still holding the **shovel** she had obviously used just before to fill soil into a flower pot.
But why was she sitting here on the ground? And, more importantly, what was the matter with her? Why was she so strangely absent-minded?
Justus knelt down next to Emiliano, attentively looking into the old lady's face. She didn't return his look but kept on staring at the ground. "Looks like shock," the First Detective assumed.
Suddenly the eyes of Emiliano's grandmother **flickered** briefly. Then she lifted her eyes and looked at Justus and her grandson, still quite shocked. "It's … it's all right … I'm okay," she gasped with an effort, barely **audible**. "I … I just have to … rest for a second."

---

desperation – Verzweiflung; **apron** – Schürze; **to pant** – schnaufen; **shovel** – (kleine) Schaufel; **to flicker** – aufflackern; **audible** – hörbar

"Grandma!" It was Pedro who had arrived with his grandfather in the meantime. "Why are you sitting here?" he asked anxiously, looking at his grandmother with big frightened eyes. "Come on, get back up, Grandma, please!"

"Esperanza." Pancho's voice was also trembling. "For heaven's sake, what has happened?"

"It's … it's … I don't know …" Slowly, Esperanza lifted her left arm and pointed towards the tool shed with trembling fingers. "Over … there."

"In the tool shed?" Emiliano asked her. "Was there something in the tool shed? Some animal?"

"No, not in the tool shed itself." Esperanza moved her head back and forth slowly. "There … in front of it."

"Let's go over there and take a look," Justus decided and got up. Bob and Pancho joined him. Emiliano and Pedro stayed with their grandmother.

"Bob, can you find anything strange or unusual here?" Justus asked when they stood next to the small shed. "Or you, Señor de la Cruz? Is anything different than it usually is?"

The old man shook his head, and the boys couldn't notice anything particular, either. Besides some dust, rocks and some grass, there was nothing around. The tool shed was a small **shack** without windows, nearly **rectangular**, with a **corrugated tin roof** and a door with **padlock**. The shed was locked.

"It can't be anything inside the shed that has frightened Señora de la Cruz," Bob concluded, looking at the padlock. "Otherwise, she would have hardly locked it up again."

---

shack – Bretterbude, Hütte; **rectangular** – rechteckig;
corrugated tin roof – Wellblechdach; **padlock** – Vorhängeschloss

"But there's nothing here." Justus shrugged perplexed. Then he walked around the house once. "And there's nothing behind it, either," he said when he joined the others a few seconds later. "I don't have any clue what it might have been that frightened Emiliano's grandmother so much. A few rocks, dry grass, some leaves and some twigs – I don't have any explanation."
"But this here … this wasn't here before." Pancho's face became serious. "I've never seen this **calabash** before."
The old man pointed towards the **delicate** pot made from a dried pumpkin. It stood right next to the tool shed, was bright red, had a few decorative ornaments and a **lid**. It was a normal pumpkin – nothing to be afraid of.
Justus walked up to the pot to examine the ornaments more closely. "Those are ornaments that are used a lot by the Indios," he said. "These lines here, and these symbols. Seems to me it's actually of South American origin, even though I wouldn't be able to say where exactly from. Perhaps Peru."
Behind them, Pancho was taking a deep breath with a **hissing** sound. When they turned around they could see his eyes wandering about feverishly. All of a sudden, something seemed to alarm him strongly.
"Are you okay, Señor de la Cruz?" Bob asked him.
"What? Yes … uh, yes … everything's fine," the old man replied, but it was only too visible how nervous and **agitated** he suddenly was.
Justus frowned and looked at Bob in a questioning way. But the third Detective just bit his lips and shook his head slightly, signaling that he didn't have a clue either what the old man's sud-

---

calabash – Kalebasse (Gefäß hergestellt aus einem hohlen Flaschenkürbis); **delicate** – zierlich; **lid** – Deckel; **to hiss** – zischen; **agitated** – erregt, aufgeregt

den concern was. Slightly puzzled, the boys turned towards the pumpkin again.

Justus examined the lid of the pot now when something curious **struck him**. "That's really strange," he said **hesitantly**.

"What do you mean?" Bob asked. "What is strange?"

"This owl here on the lid. Somehow it doesn't fit at all with the ..."

"Of course it does!" Pancho's voice sounded sharp and convinced.

The two boys turned towards him again. "What do you mean?" Justus asked in surprise. "Why do you think the owl belongs on the pumpkin pot? Take a look here, it was ..."

"The owl," Pancho interrupted him and nodded meaningfully, "is the bird of the night!"

Justus looked at the man puzzled. This statement confused him. He knew that the owl is a **nocturnal bird**, but what did this have to do with an Indio calabash? He could only suspect that, again, this had to do with the old man's superstition in some way. Gradually, it became clear to him what Emiliano was talking about when he mentioned those strange views his grandparents were having.

"Señor de la Cruz," Justus said, trying to set the old man at rest. "I'm afraid I don't quite understand. According to my knowledge, the owl is not necessarily a normal element of this kind of Indio art. And look at this: **contrary to** the other patterns and forms **carved** into the pumpkin, the owl has been simply painted on the surface, and that even in a pretty crude way, without much artistic skill." Justus lifted the lid of the pump-

---

sth. struck/strike so. – etwas fiel/fällt jmd. auf;
hesitantly – zögerlich; **nocturnal bird** – Nachtvogel;
contrary to – im Gegensatz zu; **carved** – geschnitzt

kin so as to show it to Pancho, but while doing so he kept on looking firmly at the old man, seeing the pot only from the corner of his eye. "Now that's definitely an argument for the fact that someone is trying …"

But as soon as the lid was off the pot a cry escaped Bob and he staggered some steps backwards. Pancho turned pale at once.

"What's the matter?" Scared, Justus looked at his friend. "Bob, what's the matter with you?"

"Hey, look at this!" Bob replied, pointing towards the pumpkin.

Justus turned around, looked into the pot – and **cringed**! The pot was literally alive with countless big black **bugs**!

"What the hell is that?" **Disgusted**, Justus stared at the bugs swarming about in the pot with a crackling sound. Most of them were totally black, but there were also a few with yellow-red stripes on their back.

"Put the lid back on, Just! Quick!" Bob yelled and stepped back further. "That's disgusting!"

Carefully, Justus slid the lid back onto the calabash. Then he got up immediately. **Involuntarily**, he wiped his neck because he suddenly had the feeling that something was crawling around there. But there was nothing.

Right that moment, Peter came around the corner of the house. He wanted to say something to Justus and Bob when he realized at once that something was not quite right with his friends. **Suspiciously**, he walked up the last few steps to them.

---

to cringe – zusammenzucken, erschaudern; **bug** – Käfer;
disgusted – angeekelt, angewidert; **involuntarily** – unwillkürlich;
suspiciously – misstrauisch

"Hello comrades – what's the matter with you?" he asked puzzled. "You're making a face as if you had **swallowed** a **toad**."
"Fits it pretty well," Bob answered and pointed towards the pumpkin. "Over there. Why don't you take a look inside?"
"Hmm," Peter was curious. Then he walked up to the pumpkin pot, lifted the lid and looked inside. But only a fraction of a second later, he dropped the lid like a hot potato. "Yuck! That's sick!" he yelled and made a disgusted grimace. "Who in the world has put these bugs there?"
"I hoped you'd be able to tell us that." Justus's eyes turned towards the street, and Peter understood at once what he was thinking of.
"If you mean the car, I have to disappoint you. All I could see was that it was a blue. But when I turned into main street it was suddenly gone. So as for the model or even the license plate – negative."
Justus nodded. "Perhaps it didn't have anything to do with these bugs here in the first place. Although: they certainly didn't show up here all by themselves."
"Burying beetles," Pancho said at that moment, and again his voice had a strange **assertive** tone to it. The three boys looked at him in surprise, but all the old man did was to stare firmly at the calabash.
"Pardon? what did you say?" Bob asked.
"Burying beetles," Pancho repeated himself. "This is not any kind of bug, these are burying beetles. And where they are, death is right around the corner." He looked over at his wife; she was still sitting on the ground. Obviously she knew exact-

---

to swallow – schlucken; **toad** – Kröte;
assertive – mit Nachdruck, bestimmt

ly what her husband was thinking right this moment, and she silently agreed.

"But Señor," Justus answered, "it's more than obvious that someone is playing a dirty trick on you." The First Detective couldn't accept the superstitious views of these two seniors. His mind was working much too logically for that. "If you ask me, it simply looks as if someone ..."

"Burying beetles!" Pancho interrupted him abruptly. "Owl! ... Calabash!" He **underpinned** his enumeration by using his fingers to count up to three. "Those signs speak a clear language. In this case I don't have to ask anybody. Death is just around the corner!"

---

to underpin – untermauern, unterstreichen

Harbingers of death

Emiliano and his grandfather took Esperanza into the house, and Pedro tripped behind them anxiously. Die drei ??? came along with them up to the veranda, but they didn't follow the de la Cruzes into the house. Instead, they waited outside. They felt that they should leave the couple alone for a while. A few chairs were standing in a corner. The three detectives took a seat and talked about what had just happened.

To them, there was no question that someone was playing some very dirty tricks on the de la Cruzes. But they didn't have any idea what the motives for this could be. They needed a lot more information about the family so as to arrive at some sensible **conclusions**.

The fact that the two seniors **were** so **prone to** superstition caused the boys some headaches as well. Not just because they themselves were realistic down-to-earth characters. They just didn't know enough about things like that, and therefore they had hardly any idea what could be interpreted – and when and why – as certain signs if one was superstitious. They still needed a lot of background information. Because it was only too obvious that, in the case of the de la Cruzes, superstition played a **crucial** role. And whatever die drei ??? thought of it – they had to deal with it.

"The **bit** with the burying beetles – well yes, somehow I can understand that," Bob said. "One can certainly draw a connection with death in some way. After all, the name of those bugs speaks for itself."

---

conclusion – Schlussfolgerung; **to be prone to sth.** – zu etw. neigen; **crucial** – wichtig, entscheidend; **bit** – Teil

"And when it comes to mythology, I know for a fact that the owl is the bird of **disaster**, death and darkness," Justus said thoughtfully.
"Mythology?" Peter paused for a moment and then asked: "You mean, the ancient Greeks had already come up with that owl thing?"
"In some way yes," Justus answered. "And many mythological elements have found their way into superstition. Why not the owl as well? That would be an explanation why Pancho considers the owl to be among the harbingers of death."
Bob added: "And Emiliano also mentioned that, for some time now, they hear an owl hooting at night around here, and that his grandparents are quite disturbed by this."
Justus nodded. "Right, third. So the owl on the lid of the pumpkin pot served as a **confirmation** for Pancho." Justus started biting his lower lip. This was a habit he had, and he did this whenever he was thinking about something intensively. "Why should a calabash be a harbinger of death?"
"Perhaps because it looks a little bit like an **urn**?" Peter suggested.
"I don't know." Justus made a skeptical face. "The old man really jumped when I mentioned South America and Peru. Before that, he was relatively calm."
"Yes, I also noticed that," Bob confirmed.
At this moment, Emiliano came out of the house again. "Here I am again," he greeted die drei ??? and ran his fingers through his hair. Now he seemed by far not as happy as he was on their arrival, but rather **exhausted** and a little depressed as well. He

---

disaster – Unheil, Verderben; **confirmation** – Bestätigung;
urn – Urne; **exhausted** – erschöpft

dropped into an old **wicker chair** and looked at the three detectives in a concerned way. "I believe now you know what I've been talking about, right?"
"How's your grandmother doing?" Peter asked instead of replying to Emiliano's question.
"She's still a little weak," the boy answered, "but she's okay, I think. It was probably the shock, most of all."
"Emiliano," Justus bent forward and put his hands together. "We really would like to help you, particularly because we believe that the things happening here are neither coincidence nor mystical or mysterious. There's a certain method to it, and there's more than meets the eye here. Someone is trying to get at you, for whatever reason. However, we have to be sure of one thing before we continue our investigations: is this really in your grandparents' interest? Are we really doing them a favor? We don't have the impression that that's the case. And of course, we cannot work on a case without the **explicit consent** of those concerned – I guess you'll understand that."
But Emiliano shook his head vigorously. "Pancho is simply terrified," he said with **determination**. "He just can't think straight any longer. He would most preferably just ignore the whole thing and wait until it is all over. But I can't accept that. You could see for yourself what happened today. It gets worse and worse, and at some point it will get even worse than someone just trying to scare us. I'm sure of that. No, something has to happen, and I'm really asking you to help us! No matter what Pancho says, help us. Please!"
Emiliano was almost begging them when he looked at each

---

wicker chair – Korbstuhl; **explicit** – ausdrücklich, klar;
consent – Zustimmung; **determination** – Entschlossenheit

of the detectives. Justus, Peter and Bob looked at each other briefly so as to come to an agreement. Then Justus said: "Okay. We'll do what we can. Maybe it'll turn out a little bit more complex than usual, but you do need help, that's more than obvious. I just hope that you don't get any trouble with your grandfather because of us."
"No way!" Emiliano waved it confidently aside. "Pancho is no problem, I'll get along with him fine, don't worry about that."
"Good." Justus took a deep breath and **sat up**. "Then please do us a favor and tell us exactly what has happened until now. Each little detail could be important. The best would be to start from the very beginning. Bob!" Justus turned towards the third Detective, but he had already pulled out his notepad.
"Ready when you are!", Bob grinned, raising his writing pad. "Alright, then let's go."
"But before I start," Emiliano said, "I have to thank you guys. I don't know what we ..."
"**Nonsense**!" Peter interrupted him. "Come on, let's get started!"
Emiliano smiled thankfully and a little bashful. Then he started his **account**.
"It all started about two weeks ago: one morning a bunch of white lilies was lying in front of our door for the first time. We counted exactly thirteen flowers. This happened two more times. Always the same number. Next was the knife. Pedro found it close to the garden door. A rusty old knife with a red handle made of glass."
"Can we take a look at it?" Justus asked.

---

to sit up – sich aufrecht hinsetzen; **nonsense** – Unsinn, Quatsch; **account** – (hier:) Bericht, Darstellung

Emiliano got up at once. "Wait a second, I'll go to get it." Then he ran into the house.
"I don't understand this lily thing," Peter said when Emiliano was gone. "And the knife thing neither. Why are those things supposed to be harbingers of death?"
Justus looked doubtful. "I'm not so sure either. The best would be to investigate this further from our headquarters later. I think the first thing we should do is to gather some general information so that we're able **to approach** the case with an open mind. If we have questions afterwards we can still ask."
Peter and Bob nodded and agreed, but the Second Detective was still unsure, mumbling "lilies … knives … ," and sighed.
Finally, Emiliano returned. "Here it is!" He gave Justus a knife and took a seat again. "That's the one. We haven't cleaned it. Grandpa said we shouldn't touch it, and he hid it from us. But I could see where he placed it."
"Hmm." The First Detective examinded it from all sides. "This is a so-called stiletto knife, a **dagger** with a long fine **blade**. And somehow it looks very old. Here, look at this ornate **hilt**." Justus pointed towards the small metal **appendages** with artistic **engravings** reaching out to either side between the rusty blade and the small handle. "They don't make stuff like that any longer these days. And look at this finely worked handle made of red glass – if it is glass. Quite unusual." He passed the stiletto on to Bob who also examined it in detail before passing it on to Peter.
"There's something written on it," the Second Detective sud-

---

to approach – (hier:) an ein Sache herangehen; **dagger** – Dolch; **blade** – Klinge; **hilt** – Schwertgriff; **appendage** – An-, Fortsatz; **engraving** – Gravierung, Verzierung

denly said. "Here, under these side parts." He held the stiletto close to his eyes – and suddenly started laughing.
"What is it?" Justus asked.
"Far from old! It reads 'Made in China', guys!"
"Excuse me?" Justus took the stiletto out of Peter's hand and checked it for himself. "**No kidding**, it's true. It says 'Made in China'!"
Bob looked thoughtful. "Who the heck throws some Chinese knife, done up to look old, into other people's gardens?"
"Who throws knives into other people's gardens at all?" Peter added.
Justus **fended it off**. "I do believe the **emphasis** is on 'old'. I can follow the knife thing as such to some degree."
"You can?" Peter was surprised.
"Hmm," Justus replied thoughtfully but didn't say anything else.
Slightly confused, Emiliano looked back and forth between the three detectives. He couldn't make any sense out of what they had said. Finally, because no one had anything else to say, he asked, slightly uncertain: "Shall I … shall I continue?"
"What? Oh yes, sorry," Justus was **yanked out** of his thoughts. "Yes, of course. By the way: would it be possible to keep the knife for a while? We'd like to investigate it further."
"Of course, sure," Emiliano replied. Then he focused on what he wanted to say and continued his account. "The next thing we had were these owls hooting. We can hear them almost each and every night, but we've never seen them. They must be

---

no kidding – im Ernst, ehrlich; **to fend sth./so. off** – etw./jem. abwehren; **emphasis** – Betonung, Schwerpunkt;
to yank out – herausziehen, hinauswerfen

somewhere around here, though, and sometimes I even think one is sitting on the roof. And the last thing happened the day before yesterday – the clock. That's when I came to you. In the middle of the night, around 1:30 – I know it exactly because I looked at my alarm clock at once – a clock was chiming seven times very clearly. But it wasn't our clock in the living room, it was a different one. It sounded much deeper and … somehow **eerie**. Later, Esperanza said to me she had heard that clock ticking for quite a while before already. Since then she's **stubbornly** believing that this was the bell of death having **tolled** for one of us. The rest," Emiliano said, pointing over his shoulder back into the garden, "you know."
Die drei ??? nodded and tried to show a certain degree of calmness. But their faces looked somehow stiff in a strange way, and none of them could deny that Emiliano's account had left them with a funny feeling in their stomach.

---

eerie – unheimlich, schaurig; **stubbornly** – hartnäckig, stur;
to toll – läuten

War council

After Emiliano had ended his account Justus, Peter and Bob said goodbye to him. They wanted to drive back to Rocky Beach and do some serious research. Then they would hold a '**war council**' in their headquarters – to gather, sort out and discuss all existing facts. And only then they would report back to Emiliano so as to discuss their further **proceedings**. Emiliano gave them his telephone number, then die drei ??? headed back home.
On their way back to Rocky Beach, none of them said a word; they were all occupied with their own thoughts. Of course, the reason for this was the mysterious events happening around the de la Cruz's house. With a grim face, Justus tried to draw conclusions, biting his lower lip vigorously. They reached the city limits but they still couldn't come up with a halfway useful explanation which would have been worth discussing.
When they passed the city limits they decided to drop Bob at the city library where he was supposed to collect as much material as possible on the subjects of superstition and popular beliefs. In the past, the third Detective had worked there part-time. So he still had close contact to the librarian Miss Bennett, who would certainly assist him with his research. In the meantime, Justus would search the Internet and organize all the facts. Peter had to **postpone** his part of the investigation for some time because he had promised his mother to help her trim the hedge.

---

war council – Kriegsrat; **proceeding** – Vorgehensweise;
to postpone sth. – etw. verschieben, zurückstellen

When the MG finally stopped in front of the library Bob got out of the car. Before he closed the car door he said: "Let's say at five o'clock in our headquarters?"
"Five is okay," Justus nodded.
"Then see you later," Bob said and gave the door a slight kick. He waited until the MG had turned around the corner, then he ran up the stairs to the library entrance.
Peter dropped Justus at the junkyard before he drove home. Of course, he would have preferred to keep on working on their case, but his mother would have **read him the riot act** if he didn't keep his promise to help her with the hedge, and she had to do it all by herself.
After arriving at the junkyard, Justus didn't immediately go to headquarters. It was already a couple of hours after lunchtime and he was very hungry. So before starting his research he wanted to make himself some sandwiches and pour himself a big glass of milk. His only hope was that he would not run into Aunt Mathilda or Uncle Titus who would have certainly found some work for him to do. But he was lucky: Aunt Mathilda was out at the hairdresser, as Bob learned from the note on the kitchen table, and Uncle Titus was noisily working in the shed in which he kept his special treasures. So Justus was able to provide himself with sandwiches and milk **undisturbed**. Well supplied, he finally sneaked into their headquarters, arranged everything he needed in front of the computer and worked on his Internet research for the hours to come.
Shortly after five, Peter and Bob showed up as agreed. "We really have to **lubricate** those door hinges," Peter said after he

---

to read so. the riot act – Redewendung für: jem. tadeln;
undisturbed – ungestört; **to lubricate sth.** – etw. ölen, schmieren

opened the trailer door with a loud squeak. **Ostentatiously**, he moved it back and forth. "Sounds horrible."
"Hmm?" Justus was still occupied with his Internet research, checking a homepage he had just opened.
"The door squeaks," Peter repeated and went to the refrigerator. He took out a carton of orange juice and **quenched** his thirst with some big gulps. "Uh! Feels good! That hedge was a pain!" Then he dropped into a chair, looking at his friends expectantly. "Let's start."
"Okay." Justus closed the homepage and turned around to his friends. "Then let's go! You start, third," he said to Bob. "What did you find out?"
"Listen, guys." The third Detective got out his notepad and started reading. "The lily is generally considered to be a flower of death and is often used at funerals. Under no circumstances should it be given to older people as a gift because lilies are also considered to be a harbinger of death. And if someone gives you lilies as a gift this could be interpreted as if he or she would like to see you dead soon. I couldn't find out though why lilies have this particular **significance** given to them."
Justus checked his own research results briefly and then said: "That matches pretty well with what I've found. What could you find out about the knife, Bob?"
"If someone finds a knife ...," Bob answered hesitantly while checking his notes, "uh, here it is. If someone finds a knife this is, according to superstition, another sign that someone close to her or him is about to die."
"Crazy!" Peter said, tapping his forehead meaningfully. "Incredible, the stuff people believe in!"

---

ostentatiously – demonstrativ, ostentativ; **to quench** – (Durst) stillen, löschen; **significance** – Bedeutung

"That's true. There are even people who believe in the existence of ghosts," Bob remarked dryly without looking up from his pad.
Peter understood the **innuendo** at once but didn't say anything. Instead, he grimaced ironically. Justus hadn't followed his friends' words; he had accessed the Internet again in the meantime and called up a page.
"I found something very interesting about the knife, the stiletto that is," he said and pointed towards the screen. "Take a look at this, guys!" Justus moved aside a little bit so that Peter and Bob could take a better look.
"Isn't that … ," Peter started.
"The same stiletto!", Bob called out loud. "It looks exactly like the de la Cruz's knife!"
"**You bet**!" Justus pulled out Emiliano's stiletto and placed it in front of the screen. "The one shown on the monitor dates back to the time of King Charles V of Spain – that's the first half of the 16th century. And our knife is an exact **replica** of this old Spanish stiletto, probably made for lovers of old weapons. On the other hand, it could be a film **prop**, or maybe it's sold as a fancy letter-opener in some shops for office supplies, who knows. In any case, it's an identical copy of a **medieval** original."
"So it is valuable after all?" Peter asked in surprise. He took the slim dagger into his hands and held it against the light which was **refracting** through the red glass handle.
"No, I don't think so," Justus answered. "I don't believe that

---

innuendo – (versteckte) Anspielung, Andeutung;
you bet! – So ist es! In der Tat! Und ob!; **replica** – Nachbildung, Kopie, Replikat; **prop** – Requisite; **medieval** – mittelalterlich;
to refract – (Licht) brechen, ablenken

someone has replicas like these produced in China if they want a high-quality product. I'm sure this is **bulk commodity**. But the question is why, of all things, a copy of this unusual stiletto and not some other knife landed in the de la Cruz's garden. Because, if it were just to cause the superstition any other knife would have served as well. So there's got to be some other meaning to it."

"Yes, but what is it?" Bob looked baffled.

Justus shook his head. Obviously he didn't have a clue, either. "I don't know. I don't have any idea."

Bob was lost in thought for a few more seconds, then he turned back to his notepad. "Well alright, let's continue for now. Maybe we'll get a sudden inspiration later on. Next thing is this owl. As you already mentioned, Just, it is considered the bird of disaster, death and darkness. Most of all, this image is due to its activities at night and its mysterious hooting. But for the old Greeks, it was a symbol of wisdom at the same time, and the bird even showed up on their coins."

"Excellent, third," Justus praised him. "I couldn't have summarized it better."

"Then we have the case with the burying beetles. I couldn't find anything about the bug having to do with superstition, but as I said before: the name as such speaks for itself **to associate** the insect with death."

"They are **scavengers**," Justus cited his notes. "Burying beetles usually gather around the cadaver of small animals such as mice, for example. With certain burying motions, the bugs then dig a hole around it so that the cadaver rolls into a ball and drops in there."

---

bulk commodity – Massenware; **to associate** – in Verbindung bringen; **scavenger** – (hier:) Aasfresser

"So now we're in the know about these creatures as well." Peter swallowed dryly.
"Which leaves us with the 'clock of death'." Bob turned back a few pages of his notepad. "Popular belief says: if someone hears a clock ticking which in fact doesn't exist, then this ticking **predicts** the death of a closely related person. Time is running out for that person, so to speak."
"That's more or less what I found, too," Justus said. "Was that it, Bob?"
The third Detective folded up his notepad and nodded. "Yep, that's it. Although – I could tell you a lot more on the subject of superstition. You wouldn't believe what kind of ideas people come up with. Hotels with no room number 13, bread forgotten in the oven, dreams of people who died long since or of teeth falling out, **withering** plants – I guess if you want to, you can interpret just about everything into any event."
"You could be right with that," Justus agreed. "Okay, so then let's ..."
"Just a second, there was something else on the subject of numbers," Peter remembered that moment. "How often did they hear that bell tolling? Seven times, right? And the number of lilies was always 13. Is there some meaning to that as well?"
"Oh yes, that's right!" Bob slapped his forehead. "Good that you mention it! The number 13 is the number of mischief and death," he recalled. "Everyone knows Friday the 13th. According to superstition, the number 13 is the most incomplete number after the perfectly complete number 12. But I couldn't find anything about the number 7. At least nothing which would associate it with death. Same goes for the pumpkin pot,

---

to predict – voraus-, vorhersagen; **to wither** – verwelken

actually. In that case, I didn't know at all where to look for data. A red pumpkin and death? What could the two possibly have in common?"

"That's how I see it, too," Justus agreed. "When it comes to the calabash, I can't come up with anything sensible, either. **It's a pity** that we didn't copy the pattern drawn on this thing. Then we might have been able to find out where it originally came from. And the only thing I found about the number 7 and the subject of death is the seven deadly sins – and that's about it."

"And let's not forget about the seven **dwarves** behind the seven hills seeing **Snow White** dying," Peter remarked and grinned.

Justus tapped his forehead angrily. "Perhaps you shouldn't play soccer so hard with your head, Second. Seems like something has gone **topsy-turvy** in there."

Peter laughed: "Speaking of soccer, a little **announcement** in advance: I won't be available tomorrow afternoon because that's the time for our final practice."

"Well all right, then let's see to it that we gather some useful ideas with the help of our results so far." Justus picked up the piece of paper which he had used to list all clues and ideas they had collected in detail. "Okay, so this is what it looks like at this point: we have a number of mysterious events, which all are supposed to announce the **imminent** death of a closely related person – at least when looking at it from a superstitious viewpoint. Then we have an older couple, Esperanza and Pan-

---

it's a pity – (es ist) schade; **dwarves (pl.)**, **dwarf (sg.)** – Zwerg(e); **Snow White** – Schneewittchen; **topsy-turvy** – durcheinander, drunter und drüber; **announcement** – Ankündigung; **imminent** – (unmittelbar) bevorstehend

cho de la Cruz, both very prone to superstition; all these events have in some way to do with them and their family. And finally, it is safe to assume that almost certainly each of these events was **staged**. Which brings us to the question: Who is doing something like that – and why?"

"Honestly guys, this all sounds like a bad joke to me," Peter said. "My **assumption** is that someone is just trying to scare the de la Cruzes big time."

"If that's the case, that person – whoever it is – is pretty tough and **tenacious**," Bob added. "And besides, I don't consider the whole thing funny at all. The shock which Emiliano's grandmother got when she saw those bugs was real. No, I believe there's more than meets the eye."

"But what could it be?" Peter wondered. "What is it about these two poor old people that someone feels he has to play such dirty tricks on them?"

"I believe that's exactly the point." Justus pointed towards Peter with his finger. "There's got to be something associated with these two seniors which makes them the target of these attacks. I'm sure the answer lies somewhere in that direction."

"And what do you suggest we should do to find an answer?" Bob asked skeptically. Putting on an **innocent** face, he asked like an actor: "Hello Señor de la Cruz, is there some dark spot in your past which perhaps you'd like to tell us about?"

Justus sighed. "Of course I know that it won't be easy. But perhaps Emiliano could help us in some way."

"If that's the case, don't you think he would have told us by now?" Peter looked at Justus in a questioning way.

---

to stage – inszenieren; **assumption** – Annahme;
tenacious – hartnäckig, stur; **innocent** – unschuldig

“Possibly. But perhaps he just wasn’t able to make these connections. And **if all else fails** we might have to try to convince Pancho into talking to us about it, after all. Anyhow – if we intend to make progress in this case we’ll have to drive out to San Fernando once more.” And talking to himself, Justus added: “Besides, this calabash still puzzles me. Why did Pancho react so strangely to it? And how does it fit into this superstition spook?”

---

if all else fails – wenn alle Stricke reißen,
wenn sonst nichts übrig bleibt

Justus makes a mistake

On the following day, the three detectives wanted to meet in the late afternoon because of Peter's final practice. But when Bob turned his VW Beetle into the Jonases' junkyard shortly after six o'clock he discovered neither Peter's MG nor his bicycle.

"Hi, Just. Isn't Peter here yet?" he asked Justus when he entered their headquarters. Once again, the First Detective sat in front of his computer and read an article about Indian ceramic **pottery** art.

"No, and he won't come, either," Justus replied **grudgingly** without looking up from the monitor. "Tactics meeting with the soccer coach at his home." His voice sounded **disapproving** as he informed Bob about the facts.

"And now?"

"Let's drive out, just the two of us." Justus closed the Internet browser. "Are you here with your Beetle?"

"Yes."

"Then let's go. Emiliano knows we're coming. I called him right after school and told him we would be at his place at around seven."

"Okay."

Bob went ahead and started the motor while Justus shut down the computer. Then he followed Bob. Leaving a small cloud of dust behind them, they finally left the junkyard.

It was almost eight when they parked in front of the de la

---

pottery – Töpferei; **grudgingly** – widerwillig, unwillig; **disapproving** – missbilligend

Cruz's house. The evening rush-hour traffic in the greater Los Angeles area **thwarted** Justus's plans to be on time. For some time they could only roll along at **walking pace**. And they couldn't inform Emiliano because they had left their cell phones at home.

Obviously, Pedro **was** already **on the lookout for** them. They had barely gotten out of the car when he jumped out of the front door and ran up to them. This time however, he wasn't barefoot but had brand-new white sneakers on his feet.

"Hello Justus!" he yelled happily and opened the garden gate for them. "Hello Peter!" Smiling brightly, he stretched out his hand to Justus. "Got a new pair of sneakers!" Proudly, he lifted his right foot – so far up that Justus could have shaken it as well.

"Hello Pedro. Great sneakers. But I'm not Peter, I'm Justus." Justus smiled at the boy and shook his hand.

Pedro dropped his foot again and looked at Bob with big eyes. "I thought you were Justus."

"No, I'm Bob."

"I thought that was the other boy, the tall slim one?"

"No, that's Peter." Involuntarily, Justus pulled in his **belly**. The last thing he wanted to happen next was Pedro calling him small and fat. "Anyhow. Is Emiliano here, too?"

"Emiliano?" Again, Pedro looked surprised; Justus and Bob almost expected the boy to ask who the heck Emiliano was. "No, he's not here."

"He's not here?"

---

to thwart sth. – etw. vereiteln, durchkreuzen, einen Strich durch die Rechnung machen; **walking pace** – Schrittgeschwindigkeit; **to be on the lookout for** – Ausschau halten nach; **belly** – Bauch

"No, he had to report back to practice. Did you already catch some thieves today?"
'This practice thing seems to be **contagious**,' Justus thought to himself, completely missing the boy's question. "When will he be back?"
"The thief?"
"What thief?" Justus looked confused.
"No, Emiliano," Bob helped him out, nodding **encouragingly** in Pedro's direction.
"No idea," he replied, turned around and hopped on one leg towards the house.
Justus and Bob looked each other in surprise. Quite obviously, something had gone wrong here.
"Shall we wait for him in the car?" Bob pointed back towards the Beetle.
"No, that would look really stupid." Justus stepped through the garden gate and waved to Bob. "Let's go inside. I don't think Pancho will kick us out. And perhaps we might be successful in getting the information we need out of him or Esperanza – if we do it **skillfully**."
Bob bit his lips. "I would be very surprised about that," he replied skeptically but followed Justus onto the premises.
Pancho wasn't particularly enthusiastic when he saw the two detectives again. Pro forma, Justus and Bob had knocked on the door which Pedro had left **ajar**, then they went through the hallway into the living room. The old man didn't even look up when they greeted him. He just mumbled something they couldn't understand and kept looking at some tiny cactuses

---

contagious – ansteckend; **encouragingly** – aufmunternd;
skillfully – geschickt; **ajar** – angelehnt, halb offen

which were placed on the table in front of him, and which he seemed to work on in some way.
Esperanza on the other hand was that much friendlier to them. "Don't pay attention to this old **crank**!", she said to the boys and came out of the kitchen. She dried her hands with a towel and heartily shook the boys' hands. "Come on in! Come on in! I just finished preparing dinner! Have a seat! Pancho!" Her voice was definitely more strict when she talked to her husband. "Clean up your stuff, dinner is ready!"
"That's very kind of you," Justus replied, and immediately he felt more at home. Sometimes, Aunt Mathilda sounded similar when she talked to Uncle Titus. Besides, Justus hadn't had dinner this evening and was glad to get something to eat. "Thank you", Bob said as well and pulled back a chair to take a seat. Contrary to Justus he wasn't hungry, but if he would turn down the invitation now they would probably never have a chance to talk to these two elders.
"Not there!" Pancho **growled** at Bob when he wanted to sit down. "*I'm* sitting there!"
"Pardon me, I didn't know …"
"Pancho!" Esperanza started to get angry with her husband now. "Either you behave yourself or you can eat your dinner out on the veranda! These are guests! *Borrico viejo!*"
That meant 'old donkey'; Justus and Bob understood that much Spanish.
"Hmm," the old man mumbled something but didn't look at his wife and kept silent. Obviously he knew quite well when he was about to overdo it.

---

crank – Griesgram, Miesepeter; **to growl** – knurren;

Dinner consisted of Chili con Carne – red beans with spiced **ground meat**. And spicy the dinner was indeed. This was a problem because the two detectives didn't get much of a chance to talk during dinner. This was due to the fact that they had to fight a terrible burning **sensation** on their tongues: whenever they weren't chewing on their food they drank large amounts of water or fanned cool air into their faces, attracting as little attention as possible.
Finally their plates were emptied – neither Justus nor Bob were particularly **keen on** a refill –, and the dessert promised by Esperanza sounded almost like **salvation**: ice cream! The old lady piled up the plates and collected the **cutlery**.
"Wait!" Justus got up and walked around the table. "I'll help you."
"Thank you, that's very kind of you! Pancho!" The way Esperanza pronounced her husband's name sounded like a **whip crack**, and the old man visibly cringed at once. "Get out the dessert bowls. First the dessert, then you can smoke!"
The old man laid his pipe aside again which he had just gotten out of his pocket, mumbled something like "Madre mia!" and got up. Grumbling, he accepted his fate.
Justus took the plates into the kitchen. It was a small room, equipped with just **the barest necessities**. Around this time, the sunset light was shining through the only window on the west side and flooded the kitchen with a warm red color. Looking out this window, one could see the flower beds and, behind the tool shed, the steppe stretching out behind San Fernando.

---

ground meat – Hackfleisch; **sensation** – Gefühl, Empfindung; **to be keen on sth.** – auf etw. erpicht sein; **salvation** – Erlösung, Rettung; **cutlery** – Besteck; **whip crack** – Peitschenhieb; **the barest necessity** – das Allernotwendigste, Nötigste

In the distance the steep jagged foothills of the mountain ridge were rising.
At first, Justus thought what he saw in the light of the sunset was an optical illusion. The last **sunbeams** already touched the mountain tops in the back, and single beams of light were shining almost horizontally on the steppe, changing the dusty landscape into a flickering and glimmering ocean of light and long shadows. It was hard to take a close look without the eyes hurting. That was why the First Detective thought at first he was fooled by a bizarre **mirage** or something similar.
But what he saw out there was no mirage! What he saw was real!
"Isn't that ... !" it escaped him. He placed the plates in the sink and walked up close to the window. "I can't believe it! Señora de la Cruz! Look! Look!"
"What's the matter? You want to show me something?" Esperanza stepped next to Justus at the window. "Something out there?" She stood on tiptoes, held one hand in front of her eyes so as to protect them from the sunlight, and looked over the curtain into the direction Justus was pointing towards.
At that moment, the First Detective realized that he had made a mistake. He should never have shown the old lady what he had seen. But now it was too late.
Sheer horror showed in Esperanza de la Cruz's face – so much that she wasn't even able to yell. For a few seconds, she kept staring out the window. Then she suddenly started staggering, briefly held on to Justus, and then sank down to the kitchen floor.

---

sunbeam – Sonnenstrahl; **mirage** – Luftspiegelung, Fata Morgana

The red knight

"Señora de la Cruz!" Justus dropped on his knees and looked at the old lady fearfully.
"Justus?" Bob called for his friend from the living room. First, he had heard the excited voice of his friend, then a **dull thud**. His instinct told him that something wasn't quite right. "Everything okay?"
"Bob, quick!" Justus sounded anxious, almost **desperate**. "Call an ambulance! Hurry up!"
"What? What happened?" Bob jumped up from the table and rushed into the kitchen. Esperanza sat leaning against a cupboard, and Justus was kneeling in front of her. The old lady was **pale as a sheet**, and big beads of sweat were visible on her forehead. Her left arm was hanging down **slackly**, and with her right hand she felt for her heart.
"For heaven's sake! Just, what happened?"
"The ambulance! Quick. I think she's had a heart attack!"
"What? A heart attack? Are you sure?"
"The symptoms clearly speak for it. But I think it's only a light one." Justus hesitated and then added: "At least I hope so."
"Abuelita!" Behind them, Pedro started **to sob**.
"Esperanza! Cariña!" Pancho pushed Bob out of the doorway and rushed towards his wife. He was just about to bend down when he accidentally looked out the kitchen window. **As if petrified**, he stopped.

---

dull thud – dumpfer Aufprall, Aufschlag; **desperate** – verzweifelt;
pale as a sheet – kreidebleich; **slackly** – schlaff;
to sob – schluchzen; **as if petrified** – wie versteinert

Bob was surprised and headed for the window as well, but Justus called him back immediately. "The phone, Bob! Call the doctor!"
"Yes … yes of course, wait." Bob rushed back into the living room, quickly searched for the phone, and found it on the sideboard. He took it, dialed 911, and when he was connected with the emergency call operator a few seconds later, he ordered an ambulance. Then he rushed back into the kitchen.
"The ambulance is on its way," he informed Justus.
"Well done." Turning towards Esperanza, the First Detective said **soothingly**: "The ambulance will be here soon, Señora, very soon. Just keep on breathing regularly, in and out." Justus showed her how to breathe in and out rhythmically; he just couldn't think of anything else to do at that moment. "They should be here any minute."
Esperanza tried to smile, but all she could manage was a slight twitch at the corners of her mouth. She was in great pain, very visibly so.
Pancho still stood in front of the window. Unable to move, he looked out into the steppe flooded with light. He mumbled something, but Bob couldn't understand it; it was too **inarticulate** and too **low**.
The third Detective went over to Justus; perhaps he was able to help in some way, after all. On his way over, however, he briefly glanced out the window. He had to find out what was absorbing the old man's attention to such a degree.
Bob saw at once what had horrified Esperanza so much. And he also had to catch his breath on first sight.

---

soothingly – beruhigend; **inarticulate** – undeutlich;
low – (hier:) leise

Out there, less than 30 yards away, he could see a horseman. As if on a stage, he was lit by the last rays of the setting sun glowing behind one of the mountain tops. But it wasn't just any old horseman. He looked like a creature from another world, another time.
The horse was elaborately **bridled**, wearing a magnificent **crimson** blanket under red **armor** rimmed with silver and gold fittings which glinted in the sun. In this armor, it hardly looked like a horse any longer but rather like a fierce, fighting machine. This impression was made even stronger by the animal nervously **prancing** on the spot, **pawing**, **neighing** and trying to rise up on its hind legs.
But the horseman had his horse under tight control, even holding it back with only one hand. He himself also wore shining armor from head to toe which was **ablaze** in the glaring sunset as if consisting of liquid metal. The visor of the helmet was down so that the face of the horseman couldn't be seen.
Suddenly he lifted his free hand, pointed directly towards them and made his horse rise up in the air. For two or three seconds the horse was balancing on its hind legs, kicking out with its forelegs, then it came down again. In the whirled-up dust the horseman turned around and quickly took off in the direction of the sunset, so fast that the ground vibrated from the hoofbeats.
Bob had a hard time **to tear himself away from** this unreal scene.

---

to bridle – (auf)zäumen; **crimson** – purpurrot; **armor** – Rüstung, Panzerung; **to prance** – tänzeln, stolzieren; **to paw** – scharren; **to neigh** – wiehern; **ablaze** – (wie in Flammen) lodernd; **to tear oneself from** – sich losreißen von

He almost felt as if it had been a dream. "What in the world was that?" he whispered to Justus and bent down to the floor.
"No idea." The cluelessness was clearly visible in Justus's eyes.
"Hello?" Suddenly they could hear a voice in the living room. "Where are you? Justus, Bob, Peter? Are you here, too?" Emiliano was back.
"We are here!" Bob yelled. "In the kitchen."
"In the kitchen? What are you all doing ..." Emiliano appeared in the kitchen door and stopped abruptly. "Oh, my God! Grandma! No, please!" He rushed over to his grandmother. "What happened?"
Esperanza smiled weakly and looked a little more relaxed now. But she still didn't say anything.
"Your grandmother has probably suffered a slight heart attack," Justus informed Emiliano.
"A heart attack?" The boy was frightened. "But ... but why? Just like that?"
Bob shook his head. "She **was scared witless**."
"Scared? Of what?" Emiliano looked around in the kitchen. "What was it? Is it here? Was it one of these damned signs again?"
Justus was just about to answer when they could hear the siren of the ambulance coming closer. "We'll tell you later," he said to Emiliano. "For now, someone should go outside to tell the ambulance men where they are needed."
Bob jumped up at once and rushed outside. When he stepped out onto the veranda the ambulance had just stopped in front of the garden gate.
"In here!" he called the ambulance men through the open side

---

to be scared witless – zu Tode erschrocken sein

window. "She's in here!" With hasty movements he signaled them to come in.
The two medics did their job rapidly and very professionally. After a short exam in the kitchen it was clear to them that Esperanza had indeed suffered a heart attack, but they added that it wasn't really an alarming one. However, they still thought it **advisable** to take the old lady to the hospital for close supervision and some further medical exams. Within a few minutes they had prepared Esperanza so as to be able to transport her. Pancho decided to follow the ambulance with his old pickup while Emiliano and Pedro were to stay at home. Not 15 minutes after its arrival the ambulance left Oakwood Street for the hospital.
"Let's go inside," Emiliano said after the ambulance had turned the corner. His voice sounded hoarse, almost grim. "I want to know what it was that scared grandma so much."
The four boys went inside and took a seat around the dinner table in the living room. Pedro quickly rushed into his room to pick up his teddy bear. Obviously he needed some **comfort** after all this excitement.
This in turn made Bob come up with the idea that the little boy should better not listen to the conversation which was to follow. After all, he hadn't seen that horseman, and there was no reason to scare Pedro even more than he already was.
"Ahem, Emiliano," Bob said cautiously, **inconspicuously** looking at Pedro who sat on his chair with his knees pulled up and his teddy bear tightly squeezed to his chest. "Perhaps we should …"

---

advisable – ratsam, angebracht; **comfort** – (hier:) Trost;
inconspicuously – unauffällig

Emiliano understood at once. "Pedro, go into your room," he ordered his brother strictly.
"But I want …"
"It's nothing that you have to hear! Come on, let's go! I'll come to you later."
Pedro sniffed, slid down from his chair with a grumble and **shuffled** towards the door of his room. He turned around once more, though, and asked: "Can I sleep in your room tonight, Emi?"
"Yes, of course, but for now please leave." Then Emiliano turned towards Justus and Bob again. "Okay, now what happened?"
The two detectives gave him a brief account of what had happened before Emiliano had come home. And of course they told him what both of them had seen in front of the window – the red knight. Emiliano's eyes widened with horror when he learned about the eerie horseman, then he actually **collapsed** onto the table top. He lowered his head, ran through his hair with both hands and whispered again and again: "That's impossible! Unbelievable! Absolutely impossible!"
"Emiliano!" Justus touched his arm slightly. "What is impossible? What is unbelievable?"
Emiliano looked up, and a smile, both bitter and agitated, showed on his face as he said: "Antonio de Mendoza!"

---

to shuffle – (hier:) schlurfen;

to collapse – (hier:) in sich zusammensacken

Antonio de Mendoza

"Antonio de Mendoza?" Justus and Bob were speaking almost at the same time.
"Exactly, Antonio de Mendoza," Emiliano said, and acted as if this would answer all other questions.
But the opposite was the case. Justus and Bob were alarmed. Suddenly, a name had popped up and changed the dynamic of the whole thing. Was there finally something **tangible**, something that could be followed up on, and not this superstitious hocus-pocus which they just couldn't wrap their minds around? Their investigative spirits were awakened again, and they looked at the boy with all their attention.
"Emiliano, could you explain to us a little bit more in detail who this Antonio de Mendoza is and what he is all about?" Justus asked.
"It's crazy!" Emiliano slapped his flat hand on the table. "Just crazy! I just can't believe it!" **Bewildered**, the boy shook his head and sat at the table for quite a while without saying a single word.
But the two detectives didn't say anything either. They didn't want to press Emiliano too hard; at some point he would start speaking again.
"Antonio de Mendoza," Emiliano finally started, and his face looked very tired all of a sudden, "is a ghost."
"A … ghost?" The disappointment in Justus's voice couldn't be overheard.
"No, I don't mean it this way," Emiliano corrected himself. "I

---

tangible – greifbar, konkret; **bewildered** – fassungslos, bestürzt don't believe in ghosts and things like that, and whoever it was that you saw out there was surely alive and real. But to make things simple I'll just call him a ghost for now. Because, obviously he wants **to resurrect** the real Mendoza again."

"And who was this real Mendoza?" Bob asked.

"In order to answer this I have to go a little bit farther back," Emiliano replied. He took a deep breath, rubbed his eyes and began talking: "My father was an archaeologist. He had worked mainly in South America, particularly in Peru where he had led some **excavations**. Shortly before the accident I already told you about, he and his team were exploring some ruins located in the former **tribal area** of the Aimara, an old Indian people that used to live around Lake Titicaca, that is in South Peru and Bolivia."

"I remember having read something about it," Justus said thoughtfully.

"I always thought that my father's work was very exciting," Emiliano continued, and his gaze drifted into the far distance. "Most of the time, I just couldn't wait until he would come home and tell me what he and his team did during the day. And Dad always used to add a little **zest** to his stories, but that was something I only realized much later." A short, melancholy smile showed up on Emiliano's face. "In the versions he told me, he crawled on all fours through dark passages, **deciphered** mysterious messages, opened the lid of a **coffin** in the light of a flickering candle, of course with a loud and eerie

---

to resurrect (sth.) – (etw.) wieder aufleben lassen, wiederauferstehen; **excavation** – Ausgrabung; **tribal area** – Stammesgebiet;
zest – Würze, Reiz, Spannung; **to decipher sth.** – etw. entschlüsseln, dechiffrieren; **coffin** – Sarg

creak, barely escaped some deadly traps, and so on. I still remember how I sat on the edge of my bed every time, my teeth **chattering**, breathless and terrified. Often, my mom came in and criticized my dad for telling me those horror stories. But as soon as she did I always **urged** my dad, 'keep going, Dad, continue!' though I knew I wouldn't be able to fall asleep for several hours."

Justus and Bob laughed slightly, but it also sounded a little sad somehow.

"Well, yes." Emiliano lifted his hand and made a gesture of resignation which indicated more clearly than any words, that those times were gone forever. "Dad even took me along a few times. Then I was allowed to dig around a little like him, but of course only in places where there was nothing more to find. And I never saw any chambers, coffins or deadly traps, either. But there was *one* time when something very strange happened."

Bob felt the hairs on the back of his neck rise. In the meantime, dusk had fallen, and it had become quite dark in the room. The fading daylight produced unreal shadows. Once, a large bird seemed to fly by outside, but Bob wasn't certain. Curious, he turned towards Emiliano again to follow his account.

"It was a Saturday. I know it so well because we had no school on Saturdays. Right after breakfast we drove out to the excavation site." Lost in his own thoughts, Emiliano played with the **fringes** of the tablecloth. "Suddenly – it wasn't even half an hour after we had arrived – one of my dad's assistants called out to let the others know that he had discovered something strange. They all rushed over to him, and it turned out that he

---

to chatter – klappern; **to urge** – drängen; **fringe** – (hier:) Franse

had found a completely untouched **tomb** in a cave which had been closed. They excavated the entrance, and some symbols and letters became visible. But when one of the native assistants saw these signs he completely freaked out and yelled that we should instantly leave the tomb alone, and that we must not open it under any circumstances. According to him it was **cursed**, and would strike all of us if we didn't stop the excavation at once. But of course this couldn't keep my father from continuing, quite the contrary. Now Dad wanted to explore this mysterious chamber even more. Before doing so, however, he decided to send me home. I was very angry about that."

"Because of the curse? Did your father believe in it?" Involuntarily, Bob had started to whisper, but his voice still seemed very loud to him.

"No, not because of the curse," Emiliano replied. "I assume he wanted to prevent me from seeing something which would have horrified me too much. At any rate, I protested and refused outright to leave, but Dad just wouldn't **give in**. I had to leave, and one of his assistants drove me home. That night, my dad was very **tight-lipped**. I wanted him to tell me what they had discovered. But all he said in return was that we would have to postpone it to the next day. Then he said goodnight to me." Emiliano paused for a second, then he ended with a lower voice: "That was the last time that I saw my father. The next day he and my mom wanted to pick up an old friend who had come to visit us. To do this, they had to take a narrow mountain pass to a small airfield nearby. Pedro, who was just a baby,

---

tomb – Grab(anlage); **cursed** – verflucht;
to give in – nachgeben, einlenken;
to be tight-lipped – wortkarg, verschlossen sein

and I were still sleeping when they left. Around noon someone from the local police came by and told us ..." Emiliano interrupted his account. His fingers let go of the fringes of the tablecloth and cramped into a fist. He was breathing faster but didn't say anything else.

Justus and Bob kept silent as well. Now was not the suitable moment to ask further questions. Recalling the time when his parents were still alive had caused an emotional **upheaval** within Emiliano. That was unmistakable. First of all he had to stabilize himself; he would probably continue his account once he was ready for it. In addition, they had **to digest** the information given by him so far. What was the connection between the whole story and the case at hand? And what did it have to do with this Antonio de Mendoza?

Suddenly Emiliano got up without saying a word and disappeared in the kitchen for a few seconds. When he returned he had three glasses of water in his hands. He placed two of them in front of Justus and Bob, took a seat and a big gulp out of his own glass. Then he continued: "The tomb which my father excavated and opened belonged to a Spanish **conquistador** who started to make trouble in Peru around 1540 as one of the many **successors** of Francisco Pizarro and Diego de Almagro. His name was Antonio de Mendoza, and he died in May 1552. That's at least what it said on the lid of the coffin in which they found a male skeleton in red armor, some weapons, bits of **equine** armor in the same color, and some other burial objects. But there was something else they discovered in the tomb:

---

upheaval – Aufruhr, Bewegung, Rührung; **to digest** – verdauen, verarbeiten; **conquistador** – Konquistador, Eroberer; **successor** – Nachfolger; **equine** – Pferde-, pferdeartig

strewn around the coffin, there were the skeletal remanins of at least five other men and women. The assumption is that Antonio had taken his servants along with him into the tomb – alive that is."

Bob was just about to take a **sip** from his glass when Emiliano spoke his last words. Shocked, he placed the glass back on the table; suddenly he wasn't thirsty anymore although his throat was dry as a desert.

"He … what?" Justus cleared his throat as his voice failed him. "He took his servants along with him into the tomb – alive?"

"This Antonio was a leader of **mercenaries**, and a quite **unscrupulous** and brutal one at that," Emiliano replied. "A **cutthroat** and a bandit."

"My oh my!" Justus puffed up his cheeks, **exhaled** quite audibly and rolled his eyeballs. "That's about the most **gruesome** story I've ever heard!" Then he took a big gulp to wash down the horror that had gripped him during Emiliano's account.

"And how did you find out about all this?" Bob had got his voice back, in the meantime as well. "I mean, you were not present when they opened the tomb, right?"

"Well, about a year ago I accidentally stumbled over an old cardboard box which Pancho had hidden in the **attic**. And in it I found all kinds of newspaper articles, scientific reports and essays on the accident, Antonio de Mendoza and the opening of the tomb. My assumption is that Pancho somehow heard of the curse thing and immediately thought that it had some-

---

sip – (kleiner) Schluck; **mercenary** – Söldner;
unscrupulous – skrupellos, gewissenlos;
cutthroat – Halsabschneider; **to exhale** – ausatmen;
gruesome – grauenhaft, grauenvoll; **attic** – Dachboden, -kammer

thing to do with mom's and dad's death. By now you know how he ticks. Anyhow, he collected everything about the incident that he could possibly get a hold of, and put it into this box."

"So your grandparents know about this Antonio de Mendoza," Justus said thoughtfully and more to himself.

"Oh yes, they do." Emiliano sighed.

"That could explain why your grandfather reacted so strangely to the pumpkin pot. Perhaps that was already enough to remind him of Antonio."

"And the knife!" Bob remembered. "The knife, or rather the original, dates from exactly the time period when this Antonio was alive. This can't be pure coincidence!"

Emiliano shrugged. "It could very well be that Pancho and Esperanza **entertained the suspicion** that Antonio's curse would now fulfill itself. That would be like them."

"Now let's get back to the curse once more." Bob held on to his glass, slightly bending over the table. "You already mentioned that one of the natives said something to that degree before they opened the tomb. What did he actually mean with it?"

Emiliano's look turned into a fixed gaze again. "I don't know what that man meant. Perhaps there is some old tribal belief he suddenly remembered. Because it was impossible for him to know about the **tablet** in the tomb – at that time, it still hadn't been opened."

"A tablet? There was some tablet in the tomb?" In the half-light Bob was searching for Emiliano's eyes. "You mean one of these stone tablets with something written on it, or something of the sort?"

---

to entertain a suspicion – Verdacht hegen;
tablet – Tafel

Emiliano nodded. "The **gist** of what it said was as follows. I still remember very well because it really horrified me when I read it for the first time: whoever should disturb Antonio's **sepulchral peace** or rob his treasures would be cursed and **doomed** for eternity. But the curse wasn't limited to just the **tomb raider**: Antonio has also cursed all **descendants** of the raider – all the way down to the 20th generation. So mathematically, the curse is still in force."
Again, the boys were silent for quite some time. And just as Justus was about to say something they suddenly heard an eerie sound: the hooting of an owl!

---

gist – Hauptinhalt, -punkt; **sepulchral peace** – Grabruhe;
to doom – verdammen, verurteilen; **tomb raider** – Grabschänder;
descendant – Nachkomme

The mercenary's curse

"Someone makes a bloodthirsty Spanish robber-knight who has been dead for more than four hundred years and is buried thousands of miles away come to life again?" Confused, Peter scratched his head. "But what for? And what does this have to do with these **portents** of death?"
"I was also thinking about this question all morning, and I collected some **theses** which might help to sheed some light on the case." Justus pulled a large notepad out of his school bag and opened it.
"Did you have a free period or something?" Surprised, Peter pointed towards the closely written page.
"No, why?"
"When did you write this?"
"During math and physics." Justus's look showed that he didn't really know what the problem was.
"Uh yes." Peter smiled vaguely. "I forgot that school doesn't occupy you nearly as much as us **mortals**. Well then, go on, super brain."
Justus looked at his friend, grimaced, and nodded in agreement. "So listen, guys," he started. "I can imagine the following three scenarios. All of them deal with the subject of **revenge** in one way or another. First: a former colleague of Emiliano's father is behind this spook. Perhaps Señor de la Cruz had **cheated him** at some point in time, or he managed to get the

---

portent – (böses) Omen; **theses (pl.), thesis (sg.)** – These(n);
mortal – Normalsterblicher; **revenge** – Rache, Vergeltung;
to cheat so. – jmd. übervorteilen, prellen

lead in an excavation, or he pretended some findings were his when in fact they weren't, or something of the sort. And it doesn't even have to have been an **evil** intention on the part of Emiliano's father. Perhaps this colleague was just **envious**, or he felt disadvantaged somehow though he didn't have a reason to, or he felt his pride as a scientist injured – something along these lines. And now he wants to take revenge for his spoiled career by driving the remaining de la Cruz family members crazy with this superstition **racket**."

"Hmm." Bob looked at Justus skeptically.

"What, 'hmm'? Could be, after all!"

"After six years? That's how long ago the accident was. I don't know."

"Seems rather unlikely to me as well, this version," Peter agreed with Bob. "Besides – how does the guy know that Emiliano's grandparents are into this kind of superstition?"

"Well yes, I agree," Justus replied, "some additional factors would be needed to complete this thesis. For example, this colleague would have had to have taken a long time until he finally tracked down the remaining de la Cruz family members – something that, I believe, shouldn't have been so hard for him, after all. Or he had been imprisoned and was just recently released, or this ..."

Peter nodded, pretending to understand. "And the second scenario?"

Justus looked at his friend in an **ungracious** way. He just couldn't stand it when he got interrupted during his explanations or, worse, when he wasn't taken seriously. But basically, he himself didn't really believe in the theory with the colleague,

---

evil – böse; **envious** – neidisch; **racket** – Spektakel, Lärm, unlauteres Unternehmen; **ungracious** – ungnädig;

either. "Well alright, so we drop it. The second scenario is based on the assumption that Indios are behind the events happening around the de la Cruz's home – that is, those Indios living near Antonio's tomb. Remember that this native was scared to death at the mere thought of opening the tomb. Now that the tomb is open, these Indios are perhaps afraid that they will become the target of the curse. And the only way to prevent this, according to their belief, might be **to disarm** the person who started the curse or his family members, for that matter. In a way, they want to calm down the gods of revenge by offering them a **sacrifice**."
This time, Peter and Bob didn't say anything at first but looked at Justus with slight disbelief. Was he really serious about that?
"Okay, okay, never mind." Justus quickly waved it aside. "In my view, the third scenario is the most realistic one anyway."
"Perhaps Emiliano's father accidentally excavated an ancient landing site for extraterrestrials?" Peter said with a perfectly straight face. "I heard that there are supposed to be some around in South America."
"So the third scenario ..." Justus acted as if he had not heard Peter's remark. "What if the descendants of Antonio de Mendoza are responsible for everything that happened to the de la Cruzes? What Emiliano's father has done there must seem like the **desecration** of the grave to them. Their forefather's peace was disturbed!"
Justus stretched out his arms as if Antonio would personally stand in front of them to prove his point. Peter and Bob looked thoughtfull.
The First Detective continued: "So the Mendozas, or whatev-

---

to disarm – (hier:) unschädlich machen (ugs.); **sacrifice** – Opfer
desecration – Schändung, Entweihung

er their name is now, identify the tomb raider and find out that he and his wife are not alive anymore. So they find the family members still alive and bring terror into their lives. But to find all this out, and to arrange everything, that could have taken them a long time indeed. Besides, we don't know when they learned about the opening of the tomb. But eventually they might have gathered all the information required, made their preparations, and finally they could get started. They had **to restore** the honor of the de Mendoza family! And if you will, they now take revenge by **paying back in the same coin**: for Antonio's lost sepulchral peace the de la Cruzes must live in the terrible uncertainty whether one of them will die soon! Well, what do you think?" Justus looked at his friends expectantly.
Peter didn't look quite as skeptical as before but he was far from convinced. "And you assume they take revenge by staging this superstition spook?" he said after a while.
"If they know that the de la Cruzes are into something like that it would obviously be an idea, or don't you think so?"
"And how would they be able to get that information?"
"I don't think it's that hard to find out," Justus pointed out. "You just visit them incognito, or you talk to the neighbors, or you call them on the phone using some **false pretenses** – there are always ways and means to identify a person's weak spots."
"Oh well." Peter shook his head in disbelief. "The point concerning this 'sepulchral peace' sounded pretty queer to me at first, but yes, on the whole this might be the most reasonable scenario."

---

to restore sth. – etw. wieder herstellen; **to pay back in the same coin** – mit Gleichem heimzahlen, vergelten; **false pretenses** – falsche Vorwände

"I agree," Bob said. "Sounds logical indeed. And it would fit in with what I found about Antonio and the excavations at the library."
"You were at the library in between?" Peter was surprised. "When was that? During math and physics as well?"
Bob patted his belly with one hand. "Very simple – I skipped lunch." Then he reached for the folder which Peter saw on the carrier of his bicycle and pulled out a few pieces of paper.
"First of all," the third Detective started, "everything that Emiliano has told us **corresponds** with what I've found. The place of the tomb, the name Antonio de Mendoza, the story about the skeletons and the tablet – it's all identical. There was hardly any information on the subject at our local library, so I contacted Stanford University in Palo Alto. They copied and faxed me an article from an archeological magazine which illustrates the events precisely and in all details. Here!" Bob put a small stack of paper on the desk, tapping on its top with one finger. "This article contains everything known about the opening of the tomb at this time. And with regard to Justus's thesis, it is very interesting that all the experts, and the public as well, were not informed in detail about it until only three years ago. You can read it here." Bob pointed to a section of the article which he had highlighted with a yellow marker. "Now this doesn't necessarily mean that the Mendozas didn't know about it until then, either, but it could be the case, and it would also explain why it took them such a long time after the accident to become active – contrary to a colleague of Emiliano's father who of course would have known about it much earlier."

---

to correspond – übereinstimmen

"Good job, third!" Justus **clicked his tongue in appreciation**. "Oh!" Peter looked at his watch and got up. "Guys, I'm afraid we have to continue at a later point. I have to leave right away! The game begins in an hour, and I still have to go home, change and do some warm-up exercises."
Justus and Bob looked at their watches as well and nodded. "Alright," Justus said and got up. "Let's go."
Bob collected the sheets of paper on the table. "Then let's escort our soccer star to the stadium. Time for him to go up against his opponents like a hurricane!" he announced and grinned meaningfully.
"Go ahead and make my day!" Peter couldn't laugh about Bob's remarks at all. He already **had the jitters** at the mere thought of meeting El Torbellino on the soccer field.
"Just a second!" Justus stopped Bob. He took the top page of the faxed article and looked at it with raised eyebrows. "Bob, this crown on the top sheet – do you have any idea how it found its way on there?"
Bob looked at the small crown which was drawn in the right **margin** of the copy, obviously with a pencil. Peter came up to him and looked at the drawing as well. It was a rather plain sketch, the crown was drawn in a very simple way but showed unmistakable **peculiarities**. **Spheres** on top of the spikes, for example, and a broad shield on the front face.

---

to click one's tongue – mit der Zunge schnalzen;
in appreciation – anerkennend;
to have the jitters – Bammel haben;
margin – (hier:) Seitenrand; **peculiarity** – Besonderheit;
sphere – (hier:) Kugel

"No idea." Bob shook his head. "I also noticed it before. It was already on the copy when the sheets came out the fax machine."
Peter didn't say anything but looked at the crown thoughtfully and a little uncertain.
"Strange," Justus mumbled and pulled his eyebrows together, "very strange."

El Torbellino

"Okay, guys!" Peter locked the MG, grabbed his gigantic sports bag and nodded towards his friends. "Keep your fingers crossed for me." But he himself didn't show much confidence.
"Well, come on, Second, don't make a face like that. Everything will turn out fine, you'll see!" Bob raised his thumb and nodded encouragingly.
With a friendly gesture, Justus patted Peter on the back. "If your shots on goal will be the same as those which you recently bombarded me with in the junkyard, I would worry more about the opponent's goalkeeper. Does the poor guy know what's coming his way?"
Peter tried to smile but he wasn't really successful. He seemed like someone whose name had just been called out in the dentist's waiting room. "Thank you for your sympathies, guys, I really **appreciate** it. Well then, see you later. Have fun watching!" Peter nodded once more, then he went across the parking lot towards the catacombs of the gigantic stadium.
"I think he feels a little bit like me last night, at least stomach-wise," Bob said when Peter was **out of hearing**.
"Why? What was up with your stomach yesterday?" Justus asked surprised.
Bob looked as if he were still suffering and said: "Remember the beans we had over at the de la Cruz's?"
"Yes?"
"They turned out to be a real **challenge** for my **digestive system**."

---

to appreciate – schätzen; **out of hearing** – außer Hörweite; **challenge** – Herausforderung; **digestive system** – Verdauungssystem, -apparat

Justus laughed loudly. “Then I’d suggest you do without the hotdog during half time.”
Bob nodded. “That was my idea as well. Come on, let’s go and take our seats in the stadium. I wonder what the **pre-game activities** will be.”
Justus and Bob left the MG behind and, together with dozens of other spectators, they walked towards the cashiers at the entrance. A long line of people was already waiting to get into the stadium. The **run on** this first cup final was extraordinary. It seemed as if soccer fans had come to South Gate from all directions near and far so as to see the match. Several license plates indicated that some spectators had come from places as far away as San Francisco. It took quite a while until Justus and Bob could finally enter the stadium. Right behind the entrance gate they were **thoroughly** checked by security men, and they reached their seats high up under the roof of the stadium just in time before a small rain shower set in. As it had taken them so long to get into the stadium they had missed the pre-game activities. The last cheerleaders were positioning themselves on the side of the soccer field, waiting for the teams like the rest of the spectators.
In the meantime, Peter’s problems were quite different ones. When he entered the locker room his team was already complete and ready for action. His coach Jason Bridges, not the most **even-tempered** person, **reprimanded him** for being late and told him to hurry up. Next was a short team meeting and finally their ‘commitment ritual’: the players and their coach

---

pre-game activities – (hier:) Vorprogramm;
run on sth. – (hier:) Andrang auf etw.; **thoroughly** – gründlich;
even-tempered – ausgeglichen, gelassen;
to reprimand so. – jmd. rügen, zurechtweisen

Bridges formed a circle, everyone stretched his hands forward towards the center and yelled: "One for all and all for one!" Hank, their goalkeeper, had picked up this motto in an old musketeer movie.
Then they were finally ready to go. Out into the stadium! Bridges opened the door and placed himself in the doorway. Each of the players slipped past him, and the coach patted each player encouragingly on the shoulder before he went out into the corridor.
Peter was one of the last to leave the locker room. Nervous like a racehorse before the start, he tripped on the spot and looked over the shoulders of his teammates and out the door. Suddenly another door opened on the opposite side of the dark corridor, and the vague contours of several boys showed up. The opponent team was ready as well! They would enter the stadium together!
Two more team members went out past Bridges, then Peter stood next to him in the door.
"And don't forget your job in the **defense**!" the coach was **drumming** last minute advice **into him**. "You have to work back towards the **rear**, okay?"
"Of course, Coach!"
"Well then, go for it. Show'em!"
Peter tried to put on a grim look, received the usual pat on the shoulder from his coach and went out into the corridor. The sound of his **studs** was echoing hard and cold from the naked concrete walls. For a moment, Peter looked down. 'Don't you trip over your own feet now!' he thought to himself. The floor

---

defense – Verteidigung; **to drum sth. into so.** – jmd. etw. eintrichtern; **rear** – hinten; **studs** – Fußballstollen

was extremely slippery here. When he looked back up he briefly glanced over to the opponent's locker room and could see the first players stepping out.
But what he could see surprised him so much that he literally froze for a moment.
"Y… you? You here?"
Peter just couldn't believe who he saw and, **stunned**, he opened his eyes widely. Because one of the players of the opponent team was – Emiliano!
"Hey, Peter!", Hank whispered in his ear when he walked by. "You know El Torbellino? That's quite something!"
Peter felt as if he had been hit by a **sledgehammer**. "Wha… what? That is … ? But I don't get it … Emiliano?" At this moment, hardly anyone could have looked more surprised than Peter.
"Hello Peter." Emiliano lifted his hand slightly and smiled at Peter. But it was a tired smile and somehow also a sad one. And contrary to the Second Detective, Emiliano didn't seem the least bit surprised about their **encounter**. He hardly noticed Peter, almost overlooked him.
But he didn't know either that Peter would play in the opponent team – or did he? And if he did, why wasn't he interested in it?
But these thoughts rushed only shortly through Peter's mind. So Emiliano was El Torbellino, the legendary El Torbellino who Peter had been afraid of for weeks and weeks, who robbed him of his sleep and against whom he had imagined playing time and again! It was simply unbelievable!

---

stunned – verblüfft, verdutzt; **sledgehammer** – Vorschlaghammer; **encounter** – Begegnung

"Come on now, Peter! What are you standing around here for?" Bridges pushed Peter along the corridor. "Get out there!"
"Yes … but … Emi…"
"Get going!"
And before Peter could think twice he stumbled towards the exit gate. He looked back over his shoulder once more but Emiliano didn't look at him. Instead, he stared down to the ground, walking very slowly and seemingly focused on something.
'What the heck is going on here?' Peter asked himself. 'What's wrong with him? Why is he acting so strangely?' But then the gate opened, and the Second Detective walked out into stadium where he was hit by an ocean of colors, sounds and people up in the stands.
During his warm-ups Peter tried to find Justus and Bob in the crowd. He knew they were somewhere up in the roofed center block. But a few minutes later he gave up. It was impossible to identify the two amongst thousands of other spectators. It was a pity because he urgently wanted to direct their attention to Emiliano. But perhaps, Peter said to himself, they have already recognized him. And if they haven't, they would find out when all the players were introduced.
Each team did their warm-ups on their half of the field, and it would have looked very strange indeed if Peter were to run over to Emiliano and start a conversation with him. But he wouldn't have a chance to come into contact with Emiliano during the match. It wasn't even possible to have eye contact because they both played in the **offense** of their team and were thus playing on opposite sides of the field.

---

offense – Angriff

But there was one thing that struck Peter even from a distance, and with more minutes into the game it surprised him more and more: Emiliano, El Torbellino, played and moved as if he was just about to fall asleep, or as if someone had tied up his legs with a cord! Seemingly disoriented and unmotivated, he **crept** across the field, was hardly able to control a single ball and didn't make a single chance worth mentioning. Emiliano didn't keep at all what his **nickname** and **reputation** promised. For some reason unknown to Peter and the spectators, El Torbellino had turned into 'El Calmo'.
At half time he disappeared into the locker room so fast that Peter was once again unable to exchange a few words with him. And he was so eager to find out what in the world was going on! Because it was obvious to everyone in the stadium that something was going on indeed. Something was awfully wrong with El Torbellino!
Same picture during the second half: El Torbellino continued to be only a shadow of himself, and each time he came into contact with the ball the boos and **hisses** from the fan block of his own school increased. Some of them even loudly demanded his **substitution**.
But the sad highlight of this mystery was still to come: in the 56th minute, Peter's team took the lead with a fabulous long-distance goal shot by Mathew, their right defender – 1:0. Peter's team was able to keep that result up to a few minutes before the end of the game although Emiliano's team tried their best to escape defeat. El Torbellino still stumbled across the

---

crept, to creep – schlich, schleichen;
nickname – Spitzname; **reputation** – Ruf, Ansehen;
hiss – (hier:) Pfiff; **substitution** – (hier:) Auswechslung

field like a sleep-walker but the remaining team members tried everything.
And finally – the game was almost over and the added time was running out – they were finally rewarded for their efforts! The left offense player of the opposing team was harshly fouled in the penalty area – by exactly that Mathew who had scored the only goal so far. Penalty kick!
While the fans of the opposing team were cheering loudly the fans of Peter's team vigorously booed and hissed at the **referee**. After another rain shower, the ground was soaking wet, and according to their opinion both players had slipped. But the decision was clear and **irreversible**. The penalty kick was definitely justified.
It took a long while, though, until the crowd calmed down; boos and hisses continued for a while. Justus and Bob were also discussing whether the foul had justified a penalty kick when suddenly a strange occurrence down on the field attracted their attention: obviously, Emiliano's team couldn't agree on who should shoot the penalty kick!
The players stood around in a large group and were arguing! Suddenly, their tall blonde lead defense player broke away from the crowd and walked up to the ball. But another player shot ahead and grabbed the ball – Emiliano!
Emiliano, of all players … The entire game had more or less passed him by, and today must have been one of his worst performances ever!
His team members were grumbling loudly, the fans started to whistle, boo and hiss again – this time against their own team, however –, and the coach waved hectically from the sideline,

---

referee – Schiedsrichter; **irreversible** – unumstößlich

pointing towards the tall defense player who was obviously his choice for the penalty kick. But Emiliano didn't give in. With a grim look on his face he stomped towards the penalty spot, placed the ball on it, and went a few steps back to take a run-up.

Everyone in the stadium became silent. All pairs of eyes were fixed on Emiliano. The referee did a final check whether all the other players had left the penalty area, and then he released the ball with a loud whistle.

Emiliano hesitated for a second, then he started running. With his eyes on the ball and the goalkeeper alternately, he ran a slight curve. Hank stood on the goal line like a **lurking** animal and started moving back an forth.

Emiliano was just about to hit the ball. His right leg moved back for the shot, came forward – and hit the ground with full force! As if the ball were driven by a calm breeze, it slowly rolled towards Hank, who picked it up with one hand.

---

lurking – lauernd

In the ghost's grip

"Emiliano! You are El Torbellino?"
"Say, what in the world was the matter with you?"
"Are you sick?"
"Are you injured?"
Die drei ??? bombarded the boy with their questions. They had been waiting for him for quite a while at the exit of the catacombs but Emiliano took a long time until he finally left the locker room as the last one of his team. The only person left behind him was the **janitor** who now closed the big iron gate with loudly jingling keys.
Of course, the three detectives had already been lively discussing the mysterious events of the last two hours. Just as Peter thought, Justus and Bob had discovered Emiliano at once after he had entered the stadium. And at that moment they were already more than surprised. But when the stadium speaker introduced him as 'El Torbellino' on top they were really stunned. That was a big surprise indeed!
But it was even more than that, as Justus immediately recognized. The fact that Emiliano himself was this highly praised exceptional talent **shed** a whole new **light on** the case.
But at the same time Justus and Bob realized with **astonishment** that there was not the slightest sign or indication that Emiliano was this exceptionally talented soccer player – quite the contrary. El Torbellino had been the worst player on the field by far.
And then the story with the penalty kick! Why the heck did he

---

janitor – Pförtner, Wächter; **to shed light on sth.** – Licht auf etwas werfen; **astonishment** – Erstaunen, Verwunderung

shoot that one? And why did he push himself forward so eagerly? He himself must have realized more than anyone else that he was in terrible shape!
But only Emiliano himself could give them satisfying answers to all these questions. And die drei ??? were certain that he had quite a few things to tell them.
But Emiliano didn't say anything when he met the three detectives at the exit. He seemed very depressed and didn't even say 'Hi' to them. Instead, he gave them a piece of paper without saying a single word.
"What's that?" Justus frowned and took the piece of paper out of Emiliano's hand.
The boy remained silent and just pointed at the piece of paper.
"What does it say, Just?"
"It says … " Justus **squinted** his eyes and tried to decipher the short handwritten note. "If you want your brother … to stay alive … you'd better lose the soccer match!"
"What?" Peter turned pale.
"Oh my God! Pedro? Was Pedro kidnapped?"
"Emiliano!" Justus held on to the boy's arm and looked into his face, scared. "Is that true? Did someone kidnap your brother? Do they have Pedro?"
Emiliano lifted his shoulders as if under a heavy load and looked down at the ground. "That's how it's supposed to be understood, isn't it?" he said with a soundless voice.
"These damned **scumbags**!"
"Who gave you that note? Who passed that on to you?" Justus shook the piece of paper in anger.
"Just before the match, a boy came into the locker room and

---

to squint – blinzeln, (Augen) zusammenkneifen;
scumbag – Mist-, Dreckskerl

gave it to me. I don't know him, I've never seen him before. He said it was a message from you."
"From us?" Peter **flared up**. "Is that guy **nuts** or what? We never ever ..."
"I know the message is not from you," Emiliano interrupted him. "Take a look at the signature, then you know who it is from."
"There's a signature on it?" Justus looked at the note again. "No kidding, it's true!" he suddenly said, "there's a signature! And it's – no! That's impossible ..."
"Just, please!"
Justus turned the note upside down so that Peter and Bob could read it as well.
"AdM," Peter spelled and **started**. "AdM! Isn't that ..."
"Antonio de Mendoza!" Bob whispered the name of the Spanish conquistador.
Justus looked at Emiliano and his friends with an earnest face. "Guys, either this is another one of these **crude** jokes, or someone is actually trying to fool us big time."
Peter hesitated for a second, then he said: "Then you don't think that Antonio, well I mean this Spaniard ..." Peter saw Justus's disapproving facial expression, paused for a second, and then added: "No, probably not".
"Emiliano, did you call home to find out what's up?" Bob asked and bit his lips nervously.
"No one picks up the phone," Emiliano answered, "I tried it several times right after the game. But Grandpa is in the hos-

---

to flare up – (hier:) aufbrausen, hochfahren; **nuts** – verrückt, durchgedreht; **to start** – (hier:) aufschrecken; **crude** – plump, grob, geschmacklos

pital as far as I know, and Pedro … Pedro was supposed to meet his friend Alessandro. His parents also wanted to watch the game, and they wanted to take the two boys along with them. Alessandro's brother Diego is on our team as well. No one has picked up the phone at Alessandro's house either."

"Then I suggest we drive over to your place and then to this Alessandro," Justus suggested and tried to smile confidently. "Perhaps some **jokester** just tried to scare you in this **nasty** way so as to take you out of the game. For sure, Pedro is over at his friend or back at home."

Emiliano nodded but it didn't really seem as if he shared Justus's **confidence**.

The four boys walked up to Peter's MG and got in. The Second Detective steered the car out of the parking lot and onto Tweedy Boulevard. The first few minutes none of them said a word. As for the game, it had become obvious in the meantime why Emiliano had such a terrible day. In fact, it was a miracle that he could still stand upright at all after such horrible news. And die drei ??? didn't want to bother Emiliano with their considerations about the changed situation and the case as such; they could still talk about it later on. First of all, they had to find out whether Pedro was okay.

But after a few miles Emiliano suddenly started talking on his own. "I should never have attended the game," he said in a low voice and held his hands in front of his face. "Never! Because of Grandma, to begin with! Actually, I wanted to join Grandpa on his way to the hospital, but Pancho said I couldn't let my team members down like that. Grandma is doing much better

---

jokester – (hier:) Witzbold, Spaßvogel;
nasty – scheußlich, übel, widerlich; **confidence** – Zuversicht

already, and if I wanted to I could visit her right after the game. But if I hadn't attended the game I never would have received this goddamn note! And then Pedro wouldn't have visited Alessandro. And then ..." Emiliano interrupted himself and moaned. He was close to crying and had a hard time to control himself.

Die drei ??? kept silent. Finally, Bob got a grip on himself. "Don't worry, Emiliano," he said and patted him on the back in an **awkward** way. "Everything will turn out fine, I'm sure."

But that wasn't the case.

As Alessandro's house was on their way they drove to his place first. The family had already returned from their trip, and they were sitting under the **canopy** of their veranda with cold lemonade in front of them.

Emiliano thought it would be better if he didn't go inside to ask about Pedro. "Diego will probably kick me out of the garden as soon as he sees me. I already had to listen to some harsh critisim back in the locker room," he said when they parked in front of the house. And besides, he wouldn't be able **to cope with** the possible answer that the family had no idea where Pedro was. It was better for him to wait in the car and pray that everything would turn out alright.

Therefore, Justus went into the house. But the facial expression with which he returned to the car didn't signify good news.

"Pedro never showed up here," he said in a hoarse voice when he dropped into the front passenger's seat. It was very hard for him to turn around towards the back, **let alone** to look at Emiliano. "They waited for him as long as they could, and then

---

awkward – linkisch, unbeholfen; **canopy** – Vordach, Baldachin;
to cope with sth. – mit etwas fertig werden;
let alone – geschweige denn, ganz zu schweigen von

they called you several times. But **in vain**. On their way to the stadium they even stopped by your place but they couldn't find Pedro anywhere."

Emiliano nodded but it looked as if he would fall over any second. Every inch of his body expressed concern and fear. "Let's drive over to my place," he said with a low voice.

Both houses were not more than three minutes away from each other. To the three detectives however, it seemed like an **eternity** until they finally turned into Oakwood Street and parked in front of the de la Cruz's house. Behind it, thick gray clouds moved across the sky like gigantic dirty **cotton balls.**

"His bicycle isn't here," Emiliano observed at once when they stopped in front of the house. He slipped out of the car behind Justus, jumped over the garden gate, ran towards the house and pushed against the door. It was locked!

"**Shoot**! That doesn't look good at all, guys!" Justus whispered. Peter and Bob didn't say anything. But it was very visible that they had ideas similar to Justus.

"Pedro? Pedro? Are you here?" Emiliano felt for his keys, unlocked the door and disappeared in the house. "Pedro!"

"Please!" Bob was praying when they ran across the premises. "Please!"

Peter swallowed dryly. His knees were soft as butter, and it was not the **strenuous** match that caused it.

"Pedro?" Once again, they could hear Emiliano's desperate voice from inside the house. "Pedro!" But there was no answer.

Justus stopped. "We'd better call the police right away. Does one of you have his cell phone with him?"

---

in vain – vergeblich; **eternity** – Ewigkeit; **cotton ball** – Wattebausch; **shoot!** – (hier:) Mist! Verflixt! Verdammt!; **strenuous** – anstrengend

Peter nodded. "In the car. I'll take care of that." The Second Detective ran back to his car, opened the front passenger door and pulled out a cell phone from the **glove compartment**. He dialed the number of the police, informed them of the situation and came back. "Alright. They'll be here in a few minutes."
"Good." Justus was rubbing his eyes nervously. "Let's search for **tracks** outside," he suggested. "There's no sense in us running into the house, too."
Peter pointed towards the area in front of the house. "I'll take a look around here."
"I'll take a right hand turn around the house; how about you checking the left side?" Bob asked and looked at Justus.
"Okay."
At first glance, everything was as it should be: the **stunted** trees next to the house, the parking area, the dark and wet soil of the flower beds which contrasted to the rest of the garden, and the tool shed. Die drei ??? couldn't discover anything suspicious. But when Bob walked around the tool shed he could hardly trust his eyes.
"Guys!" he yelled, excited. "Guys! Come over here! Quick!"
Within a few seconds, Justus and Peter were there.
"What's up, third?"
"Did you find something?"
Without saying a word, Bob pointed towards the ground. At the far end of the garden they saw a small white sneaker, and right next to it, in the **soggy** dust, they could clearly see some fresh deep hoof prints!

---

glove compartment – Handschuhfach; **track** – Spur;
stunted – verkrüppelt, verkümmert; **soggy** – feucht, sumpfig

"You are next!"

However, die drei ??? didn't have a chance to investigate the tracks more thoroughly. Because from the street they could hear the sound of a car and then two doors being slammed shut.
"That's probably the police," Justus guessed. "Let's go back to the front."
They ran around the house so as to meet the policemen. Both men – one of them quite corpulent, the other one half a head taller than Peter – were just stepping through the garden gate. But right at this moment a car pulled up in front of the house. Pancho was back!
"Oh no!" Justus moaned. He had hoped that Emiliano's grandfather would stay at the hospital a little longer so that they could take the necessary steps calmly and with the objectivity needed. Then they could have informed Pancho of the facts in a gentle way. But now, the First Detective was afraid, things would start to get complicated.
"What's the matter here? What happened?" With a **groan**, the old man got out of the pickup and stared at the policemen and die drei ???. The engine of the pickup was still running, and the driver's door was wide open.
"We were informed that …," the taller of the two policemen started, but at that moment Emiliano showed up on the veranda.
"Grandpa!" Emiliano jumped down the stairs and ran towards his grandfather. "Grandpa, is Pedro with you?"
"Pedro? No, why? I thought he was …" Pancho paused abrupt-

---

to groan – ächzen, stöhnen

ly and started breathing heavily. "What happened here? What's happened to Pedro? Emiliano?"
"I … I don't know," Emiliano stuttered helplessly and looked down.
"Well, we received a phone call a few minutes ago …," the policeman was trying to speak up again, but he was immediately interrupted by Pancho.
"Emiliano! Tell me at once what happened! Where is Pedro?"
Without saying anything, the boy passed the note with the disturbing message on to his grandfather. Pancho quickly glanced over it – and literally froze.
"Antonio de Mendoza!" he said in a low, hoarse voice. "I knew it! I knew it from the very beginning!"
"Señor, what is it that you have there?" The corpulent policeman pointed towards the note. "May I take a look at that?"
"No, you can't!" Pancho yelled at him.
It turned out that Justus was right with his concerns; now the situation was becoming very complicated.
Emiliano just stood around helplessly and couldn't say a single word, but Pancho refused any kind of **intervention** on the part of the police outright, and he pushed the two surprised police officers off his premises. The only way to help his grandson now, according to the old man, was 'to calm down Antonio's anger'. And the last ones who would be helpful in this matter were policemen – he spit out the last word with visibly expressed **contempt**.
Meanwhile, the three detectives tried to explain to the officers as **convincingly** as possible what had happened and why they

---

intervention – Einmischung; **contempt** – Verachtung, Geringschätzung; **convincingly** – überzeugend

were called. The three of them explained the events to the policemen, sometimes speaking at the same time, because everything had to be done fast now. They told them of the mysterious events of the last few days, of what happened at the game, of what they had just discovered near the tool shed, and what they personally thought of all this. Finally, they introduced themselves to the officers as detectives as they were all being pushed out the garden gate by Pancho.

In the end the policemen had no idea what to think of all this. Justus could literally read their minds: 'was this just some boys' joke?' they seemed to ask themselves. Perhaps this Pedro had just forgotten to tell them what he was up to, or he had just run away for a while … As crazy as the old man behaved, it wouldn't come as a surprise. And these three boys: what role did they play, after all? Perhaps they were just some **busybodies**? Chances were that they were also **off their rocker**. Or was it actually the case that a child had been kidnapped here?

These or similar thoughts must have rushed through the policemen's mind, Justus was certain. But in the end their skepticism won over their investigative spirits, and they went back to their car.

"Listen, Señor," the fat policeman said to Pancho although Pancho wasn't listening to him. "If the boy doesn't show up by tomorrow morning give us another call. Then we'll see."

"Goodbye!" Pancho slammed the garden gate shut behind them so hard that drops of water splashed from the fence. Then, without turning around again, he walked up to the veranda. He walked by die drei ??? without looking at them ei-

---

busybody – Wichtigtuer;
to be off one's rocker – nicht richtig ticken, spinnen

ther, pulled Emiliano towards himself, and disappeared inside the house with him.
The policemen were fed up and decided to leave the **dubious** place with these strange people. They smiled at the three boys awkwardly, got in their car and took off.
"Well great!" Justus wrinkled his nose sourly. "That's how simple detective work can be."
"You bet, First, you bet." Stunned, Peter shook his head.
"And now? What are we going to do now?" Bob was pretty confused, too. They had seldom had a situation as complicated as this one.
Justus thought for a moment and then said: "I'd like to take another look at these tracks back there. I think we have to assume that the sneaker lying there must be Pedro's. And maybe we have a chance to follow these tracks in some direction."
Peter and Bob nodded. Together, die drei ??? walked around the house to the tool shed once more and stopped in front of the hoof prints.
In the meantime dusk had set in, and the rather **dim** daylight was **fading** fast. But right above the mountain ridges a few single rays of sunlight broke through the clouds here and there, wandering across the steppe like gigantic fingers. It was due to these lighting conditions that they recognized now what they had missed just before.
"No kidding! Justus, you were right!" Peter pointed towards the narrow but clearly visible hoof prints stretching out straight into the steppe and getting lost between some of the gigantic cactuses. "The horseman came from there, from somewhere near the rock over there."

---

dubious – zweifelhaft; **dim** – dämmerig; **to fade** – verblassen

"Well, then let's take a look where these tracks lead to," Justus said in a resolute manner. "But we have to hurry up; daylight is fading quickly now, and if it should start raining again chances are that the tracks will be **blurred**."
Peter and Bob were just about to agree with him when all of a sudden they heard a suppressed "Pst!" behind them. Curious, they turned around. It was Emiliano.
"Where are you going?" he asked.
"Here, take a look at that," Bob replied, pointing at the sneaker and the tracks. "We want to find out where they lead to."
"That belongs to Pedro!" Emiliano cried excitedly and picked up the shoe. "I'll join you," he said with a firm voice.
"And your grandfather?"
"Uh, my grandpa!" Emiliano frowned angrily. "I can't deal with his crazy superstitious ideas right now. We have to do something."
'That's what I think, too,' Justus said to himself, but kept silent. "Well then, come along," he said, and together the four boys **headed for** the steppe.
It was a little more than half a mile across the steppe to the first steep foothills. At first, the boys were walking silently next to each other sunk in thought, but then Bob broke the silence.
"I'm still thinking about the note that you got from this boy, Emiliano. Someone wants you and your team to lose the final, and he put pressure on you by kidnapping Pedro. So far, so bad, and for sure we have to find out who is behind all this. But do you think that there is a connection between this superstition spook and the fact that you were to lose the game?"

---

blurred – verwischt, verschwommen; **to head for** – auf etw. zugehen

"That's obvious," Justus replied. "After all, we are following the tracks of this strange horseman, starting from Pedro's sneaker. So there must be some connection between Antonio, Pedro's kidnapping, and the threat connected with it." Justus kept silent for a moment, and in an unhappy voice he added: "I just don't know what."
"How about the most obvious and plausible – ever thought of that?" Peter took the initiative now. The Second Detective seemed a little uncertain, almost **meek**. "It's not really a pleasure for me to say this, and I also find it hard to imagine that there could be some truth to this consideration; but if we are looking for the person who would be most interested in Emiliano's team losing the game, wouldn't we have to start with – my team?"
"What? You mean … ?" Emiliano looked at him, scared.
Embarrassed, Peter **ducked** his head. It almost seemed as if he wanted to apologize for what he just said. "Well, after all, you are the star of the team. Taking you out of the game would be a **surefire** way to increase the chances of defeating your team."
"But what about the spook with the lilies, the knife, the pumpkin, and so on?" Bob couldn't see any connection at all there.
"I … I just don't know." The idea that one of Peter's teammates could actually be behind all this caused Peter visible discomfort.
"I think we'll have to follow up on that idea at any rate." Justus nodded **emphatically**. "But for now we should focus on this." Justus pointed towards the track which led around a large

---

meek – kleinlaut; **to duck** – sich ducken;
surefire – garantiert, todsicher; **emphatically** – nachdrücklich

rock. Behind it, to their surprise, they found a **gap** between the rocks.

They had left the steppe behind them and stood in front of the foothills of the mountain range. Steep mountain sides full of **debris**, meager **shrubs** and jagged rock faces rose up in front of them. At first glance, it looked as if the tracks would lead up the mountains. But right at the spot where the four boys were now they found the entrance to a narrow **ravine** behind a few huge rocks which seemed to lead through the mountains.

"You don't want to go in there, do you?" Peter wasn't particularly thrilled about the idea of entering a ravine just wide enough for the four of them to walk side by side.

"Do you have a better idea?" Justus shook his head in advance, and Peter shrugged. Of course they had to follow those tracks.

"Then let's go for it!" Justus waved to the others to follow him, and shortly afterward the four boys disappeared in the dim gap.

Inside it was very dark. As if someone had flipped a switch, the half-light suddenly faded. The boys could barely see in which direction they were walking, and the tracks were less and less visible as the ground became more rocky.

The chasm widened after a few feet but didn't become any lighter. The light just couldn't find its way down. The ravine turned left and right and the mountain sides and rock faces rose up **steeper** and steeper.

They had walked into the ravine about one hundred or one hundred and fifty steps when they suddenly heard a sound. That is, at first they felt it: the ground was vibrating, ever so

---

gap – Spalte, Lücke, Kluft;
debris – Geröll, Schutt; **shrub** – Busch, Gestrüpp;
ravine – Schlucht; **steep** – steil

slightly at first, but then more and more by the second. And now they could clearly hear the sound. It was –
"Hoof beats!", Peter said. "Those are hoof beats! Do you hear that? My god, do you hear that?"
The others just nodded. Of course they had heard it. And just like Peter they knew what that meant.
"Antonio! He's coming!" Emiliano whispered in horror. "And we're caught in a trap! We'll never get out of here!"
"Up this side!" Bob hissed. "We have to try it!"
"Forget it, Bob!" Justus hectically waved it aside. "Much too steep. We should see if we can hide here somewhere!"
"But where?" Peter asked in desperation. "There's no place to go! Do you want me **to vanish into thin air**? Or turn into a cactus?"
But it would have been too late even for that. Because Peter had barely finished his sentence when the red horseman appeared out of the dark of the ravine. In a wild gallop he charged around the rocks. He and his horse were surrounded by dust, and the hoof beats were echoing off the rocks like rolls of thunder.
The sheer horror in the boys' face was only too visible. They were shaking and trembling, and with a fixed stare they looked at the spooky phantom while flatening themselves against the rocks.
The horseman came closer and closer, and now he was only a few feet away from them. All of a sudden he tightened the **reins**. Within a few seconds the horse came to a stop, rose up with its front legs and came down on the rocky ground again.

---

to vanish into thin air – sich in Luft auflösen;
rein – Zügel;

Loudly **snorting**, it was nervously prancing on the spot and came dangerously close to the four boys at one point. At that moment the horseman stretched out his arm and pointed towards Emiliano.

"You!" The voice coming out of the slots of the visor sounded everything but human. "You are next!" Then he threw an object in front of the boy's feet and took off. When Justus was able to look down to the ground again he recognized a small white sneaker.

---

to snort – schnauben, schnaufen

Shadows in the night

The next day was a real **strain** for die drei ???.
It started in school, and this time it was not due to exams the boys had to go through.
After their encounter with the red horseman – and after recovering from the shock – they discussed how they should proceed all the way back to Rocky Beach.
First, they had to check the players on Peter's team – without attracting too much attention – to see if one of them could actually be behind all these events terrifying and threatening the de la Cruz family.
They could hardly imagine that one of the boys on the team had something to do with it, but there was also a chance that some **overeager** father just couldn't stand the idea of his **offspring** losing that final. They couldn't neglect motives as wild and confused as that one, even when Bob rightly pointed out that the superstitious elements of the case still couldn't be explained with it.
During recess, die drei ??? told each of Peter's team members, as **casually** as possible, that El Torbellino's brother had been kidnapped – and that *this* was the reason why the star on the opponent team had such a bad day.
The detectives thought that, if one of the players had his fingers in this evil game, chances were good that he might unwittingly show it with a thoughtless reaction or a careless comment.

---

strain – Stress, Anstrengung, Strapaze; **overeager** – übereifrig; **offspring** – Sprössling, Nachwuchs; **casually** – beiläufig, nebenbei

Of course they didn't mention that they and Emiliano had become friends nor that he was on their list of clients. Die drei ??? had enough investigative sense to know that this would have scared away anybody who knew about the de la Cruz's problems. No, they managed the whole thing very skillfully, they thought, from a psychological point of view.

They pretended to be surprised and concerned, at times also a little sensationalistic, and in between they interjected a slight note of relief, even of **malicious joy** in their comments. After all, their school team had **benefited** from the incident, and perhaps they could identify the real **villain** if he showed his pride in his **handiwork**.

But there wasn't the slightest hint or indication that one of Peter's teammates was involved in the case, or that anyone knew something about it. No one became nervous, no one **blushed**, **stuttered**, or grinned suspiciously.

The clever method of questioning which die drei ??? had planned, from a psychological viewpoint, **backfired**. All the players were truly shocked when they heard the news of the kidnapping, and to them it seemed odd how lightly Justus, Peter and Bob dealt with it.

In the end, die drei ??? had to explain to the students they had talked to, that they were just as shocked as they, and that they simply had been misunderstood.

The next thing they wanted to do – according to their plan – was to drive to Emiliano right after school. Justus had called

---

malicious joy – Schadenfreude; **to benefit** – profitieren;
villain – Übeltäter, Bösewicht; **handiwork** – Werk, Arbeit;
to blush – erröten, rot werden; **to stutter** – stottern;
to backfire – fehlschlagen, nach hinten losgehen

him very early in the morning to find out if there was any news about Pedro.
"No, nothing," Emiliano answered sadly, "but I'll give the police another call in a minute. Now they have to do something about it."
Die drei ??? hoped that, by the time school was over, there would be some positive news, so right after school they drove to San Fernando. But when they arrived at Emiliano's home the police still didn't have a single trace of Pedro.
"They'll find him, for sure!" Peter tried to lift Emiliano's spirits. But the boy just nodded without saying a word.
Their third plan led them back into the ravine where they had the encounter with the red horseman the night before. They wanted to check the place once more in bright daylight – and without panic.
Perhaps they would find some other tracks which could be examined, and which would shed some more light on this dubious affair. A piece of **fabric**, a **rivet** from the armor, or a horseshoe – if they were lucky.
"How about an entire horseman complete with horse?" Peter joked. The thought of having to return to the place where they had been scared witless the night before didn't seem pleasant to him at all.
"I'm sure that the guy **ambushed** us yesterday, and that he doesn't live in that ravine," Justus argued. "That was planned, from the hoof traces and the sneaker all the way to his spectacular performance. That won't happen a second time."
And it turned out that Justus was right. This time, the red

---

fabric – Stoff; **rivet** – Niete; **to ambush so.** – jmd. auflauern, überfallen, aus dem Hinterhalt angreifen horseman was nowhere to be seen. But neither could they find anything – no piece of fabric or metal, no horseshoe, nothing! It seemed as if no one had ever entered the ravine before them. This action didn't give them any further clues or leads; they were still in the dark.

When they returned to de la Cruz's house, Emiliano remembered: "By the way, this morning we had lilies lying in front of the door again."

He mentioned it almost casually.

"What? Lilies again? And again thirteen?" Peter wanted to know.

"No, this time there were only seven. And the owl was hooting all night long."

"Seven? Why seven, all of a sudden?" Peter asked in surprise.

"The bell of the clock tolled seven times, didn't it?" Bob remembered.

Justus shook his head. "I don't understand this," he mumbled, "I just don't get it."

Together with Emiliano, die drei ??? drove to the hospital to visit Esperanza. Emiliano wanted to visit her anyway, and the three detectives also thought it would be a good idea to pay the old lady a visit. She was supposed to be dismissed from hospital tomorrow anyway, but as a matter of **courtesy** they wanted to stop by at least once. Of course they didn't mention Pedro's disappearance with a single word.

When Peter finally dropped Justus at the junkyard after this busy day it was past ten o'clock. This time, Justus used a secret entrance to the junkyard, as the large main gate was locked, and Justus didn't want to wake anybody up that late. There was a picture of a green ocean, painted on the **timber** wall,

---

courtesy – Höflichkeit; **timber** – Holz, Balken

and it showed a ship that was about to sink, and a fish watching the ship. One fish eye was a hole into which one could reach and push aside two wooden boards. Justus pushed himself through the entrance, closed it again, and ran across the moonlit junkyard toward the house which seemed to be **snoozing** calmly and peacefully beneath the black velvet sky.

Suddenly he heard a sound. A low squeak, as if the hinges of a door were creaking somewhere.

Justus **flinched**. 'The door!' he suddenly realized, 'the door to our headquarters! But … I remember having closed it!'

He rushed across the yard towards their trailer. Everything seemed calm, there was no light. But when Justus turned the corner he saw that the door was actually wide open! And then he heard someone clearing his throat.

"Damn! Someone's in there!" he whispered to himself. The First Detective grabbed the first object at his feet – an old iron **rod** – and sneaked closer to the trailer.

Ducked down and on **tiptoes**, Justus crept towards the door. He held the iron rod tightly in his hands. Again he could hear the squeak of the door moving back and forth in the gentle night breeze.

Then he was able to take a look inside the trailer. The moonlight shining through the door and the rooftop of the trailer was enough to reveal the contours of single objects inside.

Justus crept even closer. Now he could hear some **rustling**, and for a second a weak light flared up.

Somebody in there was **ransacking** their files and records!

---

to snooze – dösen; **to flinch** – zusammenzucken; **rod** – Stange; **on tiptoes** – auf Zehenspitzen, leisen Sohlen; **rustling** – Rascheln, Geknister; **to ransack sth.** – etw. durchwühlen, durchstöbern

The First Detective thought about what to do. Should he challenge the **burglar**? But what if he was armed? Or should he hide and then follow him? And what if he should take off with a car? He couldn't yell for help and hope that Uncle Titus and Aunt Mathilda would wake up. His call would alarm the burglar, and he would be miles away by the time they could help him. But suddenly the First Detective was interrupted in his thoughts. A black shadow appeared in the entrance of the trailer, and before Justus was able to react, the burglar had discovered him in the bright moonlight!

Silent and **sleek** as a cat, the figure jumped towards him. Justus lifted the iron rod in defense but the intruder was already too close to him and rammed him aside with full force.

For a second, Justus could hold on to the shadowy man, then he staggered backwards a few steps and stumbled over some spare parts in the yard. He saw the shadow run past him and wanted to yell something.

But just at that moment, he hit his head hard on the ground.

The pain was virtually exploding in front of his eyes.

And then everything went black around him.

---

burglar – Einbrecher; **sleek** – geschmeidig (in den Bewegungen)

King of jailbreakers

From far away a telephone was ringing. It sounded as if someone had wrapped the phone in a blanket, or as if the volume of the ring tone was turned all the way down. But it just didn't stop. And even though it could barely be heard, the ring tone **penetrated** Justus's brain, each time causing a sharp pain in every nerve. It was **unbearable**. Why didn't anyone pick up the phone?

Suddenly Justus **regained consciousness**. "The telephone!" he whispered and touched the back of his head. Enormous pain **obscured** his thoughts. "The phone in our headquarters."

Still slightly dizzy, he stood up and walked towards the trailer. A quick glance at his watch told him that it was shortly before eleven o'clock. Obviously he hadn't been unconscious for a very long time.

"Here Justus Jonas of the three detectives," he moaned into the receiver. His voice appeared to him as if it was coming from a stadium loudspeaker.

"Justus, it's me, Emiliano!"

The First Detective gripped the receiver tightly.

"Emiliano?"

"Justus! Pedro is back!"

"What?" Suddenly all pain was forgotten. "Pedro? He's back?"

"Yes, the police just stopped by and dropped him at our house."

---

jailbreaker – Ausbrecher; **to penetrate sth.** – in etw. eindringen, etw. durchdringen; **unbearable** – unerträglich;
to regain consciousness – Bewusstsein wiedererlangen;
to obscure sth. – etw. vernebeln, verschleiern

Emiliano's voice sounded very relieved. "He's fine, no injuries."
"But … what happened? Did Pedro say what happened?"
"We haven't asked him yet. Right now he's sleeping. The policemen said they had already asked him some questions but he didn't know anything; it seems he noticed nothing."
Justus thought it over for a second, then he said: "Listen, we'll stop by your place tomorrow before the game. It's a holiday so there's no school, and we could be ready to go right after breakfast. Perhaps Pedro has seen or recognized something which could be of help to us."
"Okay, let's say ten?"
"Alright."
Justus said goodbye to Emiliano and hung up the phone. "He must have seen or recognized something," he mumbled grimly while getting ice cubes out of the freezer. Then he went over to the house. Silently he walked up the stairs to his room, laid down on the bed with a big ice pack, and waited for the pain in his head to stop.

"The knife and the copies?" Peter looked away from the street for a moment, turning towards Justus in surprise. "That's what the guy stole?"
"Yes, that's what was missing when I checked our headquarters this morning. He found the knife in the **drawer** under the desk, and before we had left yesterday, the copy of the article from Stanford University was still lying next to the computer."
The First Detective had called his friends in the morning, asked them to come to their headquarters, and on their way to San Fernando he told them what had happened the night be-

---

drawer – Schublade

fore. Peter and Bob were of course all excited when they heard about the raid. But the **theft** which Justus had found out about in the meantime alarmed them as well.
"I guess that's called **destruction of evidence**," Bob said and made a **morose** face.
"And you couldn't recognize who it was?" Peter asked.
"No." Justus shook his head. "It was much too dark, and besides, everything went very fast. But there might be one little clue after all, and not so uninteresting either. This morning I checked the place in the junkyard where I had the fight with this mystery man. And look here: this is what I found on the ground."
Justus held up a small metallic object. It was a pin like those that men wear on the **lapels** of their suit. And at the upper end of this pin a tiny golden crown was sparkling.
"I guess I ripped it off his clothes when I fell and tried to hold on to him, or it came off by itself. It's definitely not part of the junkyard equipment."
"Isn't that …" Bob took the pin out of Justus's hand. "That's exactly the same crown as the one which we found on the copies! The crown that someone had drawn on the margin of the article about Antonio de Mendoza!"
"On exactly the same article that got stolen last night," Justus confirmed.
"Let me have it for a second." Peter stretched out his hand, and Bob passed the pin on to him. He held it in front of his face in

---

theft – Diebstahl;
destruction of evidence – Vernichten von Beweismitteln;
morose – missmutig, verdrießlich;
lapel – Jackenaufschlag, Revers

such a way that he was able to look at the pin and the traffic at the same time. Suddenly he frowned.
"Hmm," the Second Detective muttered and wrinkled his nose. "When I first saw the drawing, I had the impression that this crown seemed familiar. But now, looking at the real object, I'm sure: I know this crown. I've seen it somewhere before. I just don't know where."
Justus took the pin back and put it into his pocket. "**By all means**, we have to find out where this thing comes from and what it stands for," he said with a firm voice. "I don't believe that this is merely a piece of jewelry. It definitely has some specific meaning, and if we could find out what we would know a lot more. But for now," he pointed towards Oakwood Street in front of them where they had to take a turn, "let's listen to what Pedro has to say."
They were lucky: Pancho wasn't there. Die drei ??? heaved a deep sigh of relief when they saw that the pickup was not in front of the house. This way, they could at least talk to Pedro without being disturbed.
But it wasn't pure coincidence that the old man was away from home. Emiliano told the boys that he scheduled their meeting **deliberately** at a time when he knew that Pancho would be at the hospital. He also felt that his grandfather wasn't much of a help in this matter.
But neither was Pedro, as it turned out soon after.
"I talked to him a little this morning," Emiliano informed the three detectives while he escorted them to Pedro's room on the upper floor, "but I don't think that he knows anything which could be of help to us."

---

by all means – auf jeden Fall, unbedingt; **deliberately** – absichtlich

"Let's see," Justus replied, "sometimes the most unimportant and meaningless details can be crucial for an investigation."
Pedro was still in bed with his **pajamas** on – red with Power Rangers all over. He was surrounded by toys, and it was obvious that he had been allowed to have breakfast in bed today, as an exception. When die drei ??? stepped in he was wiping jam off a Matchbox car.
"Hello!" He greeted the boys with a bright smile. It was hardly recognizable that he had had an extremely straining and frightening day. Only the shine in his eyes was somewhat **subdued**.
Die drei ??? greeted him back, then they started to ask him questions in a gentle way. But it soon turned out that they didn't have to be so cautious, because Pedro had absolutely no problem to talk about what had happened. Quite the contrary: he considered the whole thing a big adventure which he accidentally had gotten into.
But Emiliano was right. Indeed, his brother didn't know anything which could have helped the detectives.
"So", Justus summed up what they had heard. "A tall man, with a mask on his face like a skeleton, pulled you off your bike on the way to your friend and pushed you and your bike into a van."
"I think it was a blue one," Pedro remembered.
"Blue?" Peter looked up. "You guys remember? The van I followed up on when we had this incident with these ugly burying beetles – that was also a blue van!"
"Or red?" Pedro was saying. "Maybe green?"
Justus sighed. "Good, let's go on. The man pushed you into the

---

pajamas (pl.) – Schlafanzug, Pyjama; **subdued** – gedämpft, matt

back seat, tied you down, **gagged** you, and **blindfolded** you."
"And turned on horrible music." Pedro stuck out his tongue.
"Sad **whining** songs." The boy gave a few moaning sounds.
"Sad whining songs?" Justus looked puzzled. "Interesting. We should make a note of that," he said thoughtfully. Then he continued: "Then he brought you to a shed, freed you from your bonds and the gag, placed a large cooler with something to eat and drink next to you, and then he left you alone and locked the shed from outside. Shortly after, you started to make a hell of a noise but obviously no one heard you. At some point you fell asleep, and when you woke up again it was daytime, and once again you tried to break out."
"Yes, I was digging in the soil like this count what was his name in the movie." Pedro was digging on his blanket like a **mole**.
Justus smiled. "The Count of Monte Christo, exactly. And pretty soon you realized that you could actually dig your way out under one of the wooden walls, and when the hole was wide enough you slipped through and took off. A police patrol picked you up a little later and finally brought you home."
"In a real patrol car!" Pedro announced proudly; then slightly **offended**, he added: "But without the siren. And at first we were endlessly searching for that shed – although I told them that I had already eaten up all the food in the cooler."
Die drei ??? laughed, and Emiliano patted his brother's head. "Then take a rest now, king of jailbreakers," he said to him. "I'll let you know when we're ready to go to the stadium."
The four boys left the room, walked down the stairs, and took a seat at the table in the living room.

---

to gag – (hier:) knebeln; **to blindfold so.** – jmd. die Augen verbinden; **to whine** – jaulen, jammern; **mole** – Maulwurf; **offended** – beleidigt

"That's very strange if you ask me," Peter started. "Why is somebody kidnapping a boy and then letting him escape? Is he too stupid or what? Why is he not watching over him? That doesn't make any sense at all!"
"Especially since the second final game is still to come," Bob added.
Justus wrinkled his nose skeptically. "And the policemen couldn't find that shed after all?" he asked Emiliano.
"No. It must be somewhere in the mountains because they picked up Pedro on the road leading down from there. But so far they haven't found out where exactly it is."
The First Detective nodded. "The kidnapper is certainly not a **pro**, I think you're right, Second. It's not really a sign of professional experience if a small boy can escape that easily. We shouldn't **underestimate** him, though. There has **to be** a lot **at stake** if someone is willing to kidnap a child for his purposes."
"So you think it's not just about the final?" Bob asked.
Perplexed, Justus shrugged his shoulders.

---

pro – Kurzform für: professional, Profi; **to underestimate** – unterschätzen; **to be at stake** – auf dem Spiel stehen

Two shots dead center

An hour later they had all gathered in the living room and were just about to leave for the game. Just before they left the room, Emiliano remembered something. "Just a second, the phone," he said and walked over to a cable which was lying on the ground next to the telephone. "I **unplugged** the phone last night so Pedro wouldn't be disturbed in his sleep." He knelt down, plugged the cable back in, and then they left the house together.

In Peter's MG space became tight, but Emiliano took his brother on his lap, so Justus and Bob could still sit comfortably in the back seat. Besides, it wasn't far to the stadium. When they arrived they went to the entrance of the catacombs together. Justus, Bob and Pedro wished the two opponents the best of luck and then said goodbye. But they had just walked a few steps back when they suddenly heard an excited voice behind them.

"Emiliano! There you are! I've been looking for you all over the place!"

"Mr. Willis?" Emiliano looked at the man in surprise.

Peter knew that Willis was the coach of the opponent team.

"Here!" Willis held his cell phone out to Emiliano. "Your grandfather is on the phone. He has already called a few times. He has to talk to you urgently."

"Pancho?" Emiliano looked concerned, and die drei ??? had an uneasy feeling that this didn't mean good news. "How did my grandfather get a hold of your phone number?"

---

dead center – ins Schwarze;

to unplug – entfernen, herausziehen

"No idea. But he sounds very alarmed. Here, take it."
Emiliano took the cell phone and answered: "Abuelo?"
The three detectives and Pedro listened anxiously.
"… But fifteen minutes ago we were still … No! Wait! You're right! I had pulled out the plug because of Pedro … Yes? … What?" Suddenly Emiliano opened his eyes wide. Obviously, something had **severely** scared him. "Grandma? … Por dios! … When? … And how … They don't know? … I'm … I'm coming! I'm coming right away!"
Emiliano folded up the cell phone and passed it back to his coach. "My grandmother has suffered a **dizzy spell**," he said with a tremble in his voice. "Chances are she could suffer another heart attack. I have to go see her right away!"
"Abuelita!", Pedro was whining, and tears began to show in his eyes.
"Oh my God!" Justus and Peter said almost at the same time, and Bob held one hand in front of his mouth, shocked.
"But … but the match," Willis said, slightly confused. Then he realized that there was something more important for Emiliano now than a soccer game. "Of course," the coach corrected himself meekly, "of course you have to go see your grandmother. Yes, go ahead, go see her."
Nervous, Emiliano looked around. Obviously he was thinking about how to get out to the hospital as fast as possible. But for Bob there was no question as to who would drive him over there.
"Peter, your car keys!" The third Detective stretched out his hand, clicking his fingers. "Quick!"
"What? But why?" At first, Peter didn't understand.

---

severely – ernstlich; **dizzy spell** – Schwächeanfall

"You play, we'll take care of Emiliano."
"But I also want to ..."
"And how are you going to explain that to Coach Bridges?" Bob looked at his friend skeptically and shook his head. "The keys, Peter."
"Bob is right, Second," Justus said. "You have to play. And we'll drive Emiliano to the hospital."
Peter – still slightly unsure – nodded and pulled the car keys out of his pocket. "Well then ... good luck, Emiliano," he said and passed the keys to Bob.
"Thanks." Emiliano tried to smile but in doing so his face seemed even more concerned. "And thanks to you, too," he said to Justus and Bob.
"Nonsense, come on now." Justus pulled on his sleeve, and together they ran toward the parking lot and Peter's car.
"Bob!" Peter yelled after them. "The brakes – you have to push extra hard!" – "We don't need any!" Bob answered while taking off. But that was not what Peter wanted to hear. He would have been even more concerned if he could have seen how Bob sped his car through the city streets in the minutes to come. With roaring engine, squealing tires, and a very **generous** interpretation of speed city limits, he drove to St. Albany Hospital as fast as he could. Once he even crossed an **intersection** just as the traffic light turned red, but they were lucky – there was no police patrol around. But neither he nor Justus and Pedro or Emiliano were aware what a **breakneck** ride they were performing. All of them just thought about Esperanza and prayed that she would be all right.
They arrived at the hospital precisely at the time the game start-

---

generous – großzügig, freizügig; **intersection** – Straßenkreuzung
breakneck – halsbrecherisch

ed. However, Justus was the only one who noticed that. Bob parked the car – in the no-parking zone – and then they ran up to the third floor.

But the room where Esperanza was supposed to be in was empty! And Pancho was nowhere to be seen either.

"Abuelita?" Pedro stuck his head through the bathroom door.

"Where is she?" Emiliano asked anxiously.

Justus and Bob kept silent and exchanged a concerned look. If Esperanza wasn't here anymore she might have already been …

"Holla! There you are!"

The four boys turned around in surprise.

"Grandma! Grandpa!"

"Abuelita! Abuelo!"

"Kids!" Esperanza yelled and ran towards her grandsons with her arms stretched out wide. "How nice to see you!"

"We wanted to catch you down at the entrance," Pancho said, "but they told us that you had just taken the elevator. We must have missed each other by a few seconds."

"But I don't understand …" Emiliano let go of his grandmother and looked at her and Pancho in surprise. "I thought you had … Grandpa said that you …"

"I guess I just had too much ice cream during lunch," Esperanza interrupted her grandson and bit her lips, slightly embarrassed. "Because it was my last day in the hospital, the nurse gave me a **second helping** – because I just love chocolate ice cream, you know. Shortly after, I felt very sick and dizzy, and I called for the doctor. He probably was afraid of the worst case, and he immediately sent me to the **intensive care unit**, and the nurse called Pancho."

---

second helping – zweite, doppelte Portion, Nachschlag;
intensive care unit – Intensivstation

At first, Emiliano frowned, slightly puzzled, but then he laughed with relief. Justus and Bob started laughing, too – only Pedro didn't quite seem to understand what was so funny for the others, and he looked from one to the other in confusion.
"And I," Pancho added, "I almost drove the **directory assistance** crazy until I finally got a hold of you in the stadium." It was clear how embarrassed he felt about the whole thing now. "I couldn't get a hold of you at home, and then I remembered that you probably were already on your way to ..."
"Oh, Pancho, you can tell the boy all the details later on," Esperanza interrupted her husband. "Come on, you have to drive back fast. The game is about to start!"
"The game has started already," Emiliano replied, unhappily.
"What? Well then, go, go, go!" The old lady chased the boys toward the door like chickens. "Show'em, Querido! Score a goal for your old Abuela!"
"Two goals at least, Abuelita, two!" Emiliano was joking, and laughing happily, the four boys ran along the corridor to the stairs.
The ride back to the stadium was just as wild as their trip to the hospital. But unfortunately they had to drive around some **road works**, and then they got stuck in a traffic jam. There was an accident near the intersection in front of them. When Bob finally pulled into the parking lot with squealing tires, only twenty minutes were left in the game.
Emiliano jumped out of the car, said "See you later!" to the others, and took off. While running, he pulled off his shirt and disappeared in the catacombs.

---

directory assistance – Telefonauskunft;
road works – Straßenbaustelle

Justus, Bob and Pedro also hurried up to take their seats in the stadium. At least they wanted to see the end of the game. And they were still on the way to their seats when they could hear Emiliano being called out as replacement for one of his team members. Their fans were cheering; obviously they had already forgiven Emiliano his terrible performance in the first game. The score was still 0:0. If nothing changed, Peter's team would win the final. But three minutes before the end, Emiliano kept the first part of his promise to Esperanza. With a fabulous shot from the left corner of the penalty area he scored the 1:0 for his team.
"That means over time, right?" Justus asked Bob.
"Fifteen minutes! Two times!" Pedro, who was jumping up and down nervously, answered him.
Justus nodded towards him, and while doing so he discovered a copy of the stadium magazine lying on Pedro's seat. He looked around to see if someone had just put it down for a second. But it didn't seem to belong to anybody, so he took it and started looking through it.
Now the over time started. The match went back and forth, a real thriller with countless penalty area plays, great duels, and many scoring chances on both sides. Especially Peter and Emiliano dominated the game, causing the spectators, time and again, to applaud wildly.
The only one who didn't seem to be affected by all this was Justus. He didn't seem to register any longer what was happening on the field because he was completely **absorbed** in the stadium magazine. He had begun to bite his lower lip again. Something in the magazine seemed to have attracted his at-

---

absorbed – (hier:) vertieft

tention very much. Bob and Pedro didn't realize it because they only had eyes for the thrilling match, just like the thousand other spectators.
The first half of the over time didn't result in any further goals so that everybody was waiting **in suspense** for the second over time. The game became increasingly dramatic. Emiliano's team started to dominate more and more. Again and again they attacked the opponent's goal, and in the end Peter had to join the defense of his team in order to **strengthen** it. All he and his team could think of now was to keep the score the same until the end of the over time, and then hope to be lucky in the **penalty shootout**.
But then it happened – two minutes before the end. Emiliano had taken over the ball on the right side and entered the penalty area. Peter came up and placed himself in front of Emiliano, and for three, four seconds they were facing each other like animals ready for a fight. Emiliano pretended a move towards the left – but then suddenly turned right to get around Peter. Peter noticed the **feint** too late, turned around, jumped for the ball with his left leg stretched out – and fouled Emiliano in the penalty area!
Of course, Emiliano was awarded a penalty kick at once, and Peter, who had been given yellow card already, was sent off the field!
A **roar** went through the stadium! This had to be the crucial moment, the final decision! While Peter left the field like a beaten-up dog, Emiliano took the ball and placed it on the penalty spot.

---

in suspense – angespannt; **to strengthen** – stärken, verbessern; **penalty shootout** – Elfmeterschießen; **feint** – Finte, Vortäuschung; **roar** – Aufschrei

Bob jumped up, **tearing his hair,** while Pedro **yelled encouragement to** his brother. Nobody was sitting any longer – except for Justus. The First Detective seemed to be in a trance-like condition, staring at nothing else but the magazine. Stiff and tense, he was turning the pages, breathing heavier and heavier all the time.
Emiliano took a run-up. As with the last penalty kick, he made a slight curve. The spectators held their breath, and Hank started shifting his weight on the goal line again.
Then Emiliano hit the ball – with maximum force. With incredible speed the ball went whizzing into the upper right angle of the goal. Hank had guessed the corner correctly and stretched out his arms as far as he could. But he didn't have a chance against Emiliano's excellently placed shot.
The ball hit the net, and thousands of people started cheering frenetically. And just as everybody yelled "Gooaal!" Justus jumped up from his seat, yelling: "Yeah! I've got it!"

---

to tear one's hair – sich die Haare raufen;
to yell encouragement to so. – jmd. anfeuern

A royal villain

The de la Cruz's living room was overcrowded. Apart from Emiliano and his family as well as die drei ???, there were five other men in the room, but at the dinner table there was only room for the men, the old couple and Emiliano. Pedro and the three detectives had to take their seats in the background.
All of the men present made a very respectable and businesslike impression. They were all dressed in **muted** business suits with matching ties, the smell of eau de toilette and aftershave was in the air, and each one of them carried a **briefcase**, put on the floor next to them.
But at this moment none of them said a word because they were anxiously looking at Pancho and Esperanza.
The couple had four letters addressed to them in their hands. They looked them over together once more.
The letters were all very similar. Each one consisted of a short cover letter, a list of various points of argument, and a final clause with just enough space below for a signature.
The only clearly visible difference were the letterheads. They showed different emblems, logos, and symbols. And one of the letters had a thick red frame with ornaments.
Much to the surprise of the men, it didn't even take half a minute for Pancho and his wife to come to an agreement.
They nodded at each other briefly, pulled out one of the letters and placed it in front of them on the table. "That's your club, Emiliano," Pancho said to his grandson and seemed very determined. "Your grandmother and I would like you to join *that* club."

---

muted – gedeckt (Farben); **briefcase** – Aktentasche

The men groaned, sighed, their faces expressed disbelief, they shook their heads in disagreement, and rolled their eyes in anger – the couple's decision **created** quite **a stir** amongst them.
"What? But … You can't …"
"No! You can't be serious about …"
"Please, you have to … you … here, take a look!"
Three of the men present were very excited. Wildly gesticulating, they tried to talk the couple out of their decision, holding up their own letters, and frequently interrupting each other.
The other two men, one of them a very good-looking southern European with a little ring in his ear, the other a little older with gray hair, seemed to be **unaffected** by the decision of the couple. But while the older one closely followed the excitement of the other men present, the face of the southern European man showed a **self-contented** smile.
"But please listen, Señor de la Cruz," one of the men began again, a blond muscleman with a square shaped, **shaven** head. "Why don't you take another look at what we …"
"We've made up our minds," Pancho interrupted him, vigorously shaking his head. "You don't have to put yourself out any longer."
The baldhead lifted his hand in despair, and one of the other men was just about to say something when, all of a sudden, Justus's voice sounded from the background:
"And I can tell you exactly how the couple has arrived at their decision."

---

to create a stir – Unruhe verbreiten;
unaffected – (hier:) unbeeindruckt;
self-contented – selbstzufrieden; **shaven** – kahlrasiert

Everyone at the table, except for the gray-haired man and Emiliano, turned around and looked at him with wide-open eyes. The First Detective, however, smiled calmly and nodded.
"You can … what?" A brown-haired man with green eyes and a large hooked nose looked up in surprise.
"Yes, I can explain to you why Señora and Señor de la Cruz decided that Emiliano should, of all clubs, join *Real Lisbon*," Justus confirmed.
Excited voices filled the room. Justus's comment created quite a confusion around the table.
"Oh yes? And how is that?"
The last of the remaining club agents looked Justus skeptically up an down.
"That's what I'd also like to know," Pancho said with a grim voice.
The First Detective walked up to the table. Peter and Bob followed him. "If you really want me to answer that question I have to go a little farther back in time – may I?"
Justus indicated that he needed a little space at the table, and then he pushed his chair in between the southern European and the one with the hooked nose, while Peter and Bob stayed behind him. "For quite some time," he started – as several curious and disbelieving eyes closely followed him – "the de la Cruz family's life has been overshadowed by mysterious events. Events which would particularly affect people who are superstitious. All these events can be interpreted as harbingers of death: they found lilies, the flowers of death – sometimes seven, sometimes thirteen – even the numbers can be associated with death.
They found a knife which is also a sign for superstitious people that someone is about to die soon; nearly every night they heard an owl, the bird of death; then they found burying bee-

tles, a special kind of bug, the name speaks for itself; and at night, the bell of a clock which didn't exist at all – the clock of death – was tolling seven times."

Justus paused for a moment so as to give everyone present a chance to think over what he had just said. Then he looked at the old couple almost **apologetically**.

"And because Señora and Señor de la Cruz are quite superstitious people, all these events had a very dramatic effect upon them, to say the least."

Pancho frowned angrily. "I don't think you have any idea what you're talking about," he said, looking at him **fiercely**. "Perhaps ..."

"Querido!" Esperanza gently patted her husband on the arm. "It's okay. Let him finish what he has to say!"

Justus nodded at her thankfully and then continued while the men looked at him, wondering what was to come.

"At first, my friends and I," Justus pointed towards Peter and Bob, "... didn't know what we should think of all this. To us, it seemed obvious that someone was just playing a dirty trick on the couple. There was no other explanation for it. But the day before yesterday, when I ..."

"Just a second!" the muscleman interrupted him. "You and your friends? Who are you, after all? I thought you were friends of El Torbellino."

"We are," Justus replied and pulled one of their business cards out of his pocket. "But we also run a little detective agency in Rocky Beach, and Emiliano asked us to investigate the events mentioned by me – which we gladly did."

He laid the business card on the table, and the man reached for

---

apologetically – entschuldigend; **fiercely** – böse, grimmig it. Surprised, he read what it said and passed it on to his neighbor.

"So the day before yesterday," the First Detective continued, "I got a hold of the stadium magazine during the game, and I made some very interesting discoveries. For example, it said that Emiliano had already received several lucrative offers from well-known European soccer clubs. All of them would like to contract El Torbellino, the gifted talent from the USA.

Gentlemen, you know much better than I do that there's a lot of money involved in such a deal. In Europe, clubs often spend millions for players, and if there's a chance to contract such a talent **without a transfer fee** – what better deal could there be? Well, the magazine mentioned four clubs in particular who would be interested in Emiliano:

FC Birmingham, your club, Mr. Charlton," Justus looked at the bald man, "*AJ Paris,* represented by Monsieur Lagard," he looked at the man with the hooked nose, "*Olympiakos Athens*, represented by Mr. Tiriakis," he looked over to the corpulent Greek, "and finally *Real Lisbon*, the club Mr. Abelardo is working for. Everyone here hopes **to cut the deal of his life** because your **commission** for the successful engagement of Emiliano is probably very high, isn't it?"

The men mumbled, more or less in agreement with Justus's assumption. The only person not showing any reaction was the attractive southern European; he just looked at the First Detective with visible contempt. But for a second, something like

---

without a transfer fee – ablösefrei;
to cut the deal of one's life – das Geschäft seines Lebens machen;
commission – (hier:) Provision, Erfolgsbeteiligung

anger flashed up in his black eyes, yet no one except Justus recognized it.
"And who are *you*, if I may ask?" Lagard said, turning to the gray-haired man.
"We'll get to that later," Justus quickly answered and continued. "Looking over the descriptions of the clubs, I made some very interesting discoveries. I'll let you in on some. For example, the emblem of your club, Monsieur Lagard, features lilies – as we can see from the emblem on your suit as well as on your letterhead." With a gentle smile, the First Detective collected all contract letters, placed them in front of him on the table, and then pointed at the lilies at the upper margin of one of the papers. "And the emblem of *Olympiakos Athens* features the owl and the club was founded in 1913 …"
Justus deliberately emphasized the number 13 in the date and pointed at the year written on the letterhead next to the name of the club. "Birmingham exists since 1907 – remember the 7, Gentlemen! And last but not least, Birmingham's players are also called *'The Reds'* because that's the dominating color of their shirts as well as their letterhead, as you can see right here. And the color red **haunted** the de la Cruz family so often in connection with all the other horrible events that almost everyone – superstitious or not – would have developed a strong **antipathy** against this particular color. Please remember that we found a red calabash with hundreds of burying beetles inside, a red knife in the garden, and a mysterious red knight with a horse in red armor showed up as well."
Justus paused for a moment and looked around. Some faces showed interest and curiosity, but at the same time it seemed

---

to haunt – heimsuchen, verfolgen, nachstellen;
antipathy – Widerwille, Abneigung

as if none of the persons present had really understood what he was aiming at. The only person looking at him hatefully was Abelardo. But Justus didn't get **distracted**, quite the contrary. "And now we come to the most important point," he said, and his voice had a sharp sound. "In an interview in the same magazine, Emiliano explained that the decision which club he would eventually join would be made right after the finals. Then, and only then, the representatives of all clubs would be informed of his decision. But in any case he would leave the decision up to his grandparents, and the reason for this was not just that he is only sixteen. They had always been there for him, he would have total confidence in them, and he would listen to their advice only. So!" Justus tapped the letters from the clubs and then pointed at the men. "In the light of what I just said, Gentlemen, take another look at your letters and contracts. Take a look at your club blazers and ties, as well as the metal fittings on your briefcases. And now please ask yourself one question: how strong would be the influence of these mysterious omens, and the different symbols, numbers and colors associated with them, on an old, extremely superstitious couple when they are – right at the moment of their decision – confronted with exactly these symbols, numbers and colors? After all, it is one of the most important decisions for their grandson's future. What do *you* think?"
For quite some time, nobody said a word. One could almost hear the men's brains work. Pancho's facial expression had changed considerably. Just a few minutes ago, he had looked at Justus in an unfriendly and grim way. Now he seemed to be more and more puzzled.

---

distracted – abgelenkt

"Are you trying to say," Mr. Lagard finally broke the silence, "that Monsieur Abelardo, that Monsieur Abelardo here, tried to …"

"… create a more or less conscious but strong antipathy against the other clubs here? That's right!" Justus added.

"Let's look at it this way, Gentlemen: what you and your clubs have to offer – money, **accommodations**, a house for the grandparents, and so on – it's more or less the same. But the de la Cruzes don't care about a new house; their criteria for which club Emiliano should join were quite different ones! So the couple, or their **subconscious minds** for that matter, had to be manipulated – which obviously worked out great, as we see from their decision. Instinctively, and due to an unconscious antipathy against all the symbols and numbers mentioned, they decided against your clubs, Gentlemen!"

"Now that's complete nonsense!" Abelardo flared up at this moment. "Who would actually believe that …"

"… that you **intimidated** the de la Cruzes?" Peter interrupted him. "Well, think it over! Whose club was the only one not negatively affected by these events? Yours! And which club was the final choice of the de la Cruzes? Your club! And who looked for information at the University of Palo Alto so as to find out something about the de la Cruzes' family history? Someone who, by pure coincidence, has drawn this crown, the emblem of *Real Lisbon*," he tipped on the symbol showing on the letterhead of the Portuguese club, "on an article about the work of Emiliano's father, and who lost this pin with exactly the same

---

accommodation – Unterkunft;
subconscious mind – Unterbewusstsein;
to intimidate – einschüchtern

crown when he ransacked our headquarters and knocked out Justus!" Peter held the pin in front of Abelardo's face like a weapon.
The Portuguese was still smiling, but now it seemed very **tense** and **fake**. And the other men's faces turned more and more sour by the second.
"Reading that article was quite useful," Bob said with a kind of **ridicule** which could hardly be missed. "You dug out the story about Antonio de Mendoza so that the mysterious events could not be taken as a mere joke, and it helped to cover up the parallels to the signs, numbers, and emblems of the other clubs. You knew about the deep wounds and fears this whole affair had caused and is still causing the de la Cruz family. And you arranged everything in such a way that the grandparents believed Antonio has returned, making his curse come true, and taking revenge on the remaining family members. The Indio calabash, the old knife, the color red which suited you beautifully when it came to your **co-competitor**, the FC Birmingham, and – last but not least – the spooky horseman who almost scared Señora de la Cruz to death! The combination of all this was supposed to mentally drive the de la Cruz family crazy – with no other choice than to decide in favor of *your* club, Mr. Abelardo! Because your club was the only one *without* any negative associations for the superstitious de la Cruzes, isn't that interesting!"
The old couple was stunned and speechless. They couldn't believe what they had just heard.
"Let's not forget about the kidnapping of Pedro!" Justus added.

---

tense – verkrampft, angespannt; **fake** – (hier:) aufgesetzt;
ridicule – Spott, Hohn; **co-competitor** – Mitbewerber, Konkurrent

The heads of the men and the old couple turned from Bob to him, but no one said a word; they all kept listening, holding their breath. "The kidnapping was supposed **to eliminate** any remaining doubts on the part of the de la Cruzes as to whether that ghost would actually be serious about his intentions. It was lucky that Pedro was able to escape. Who knows what else you would have done with him!"

Abelardo's fake smile was completely gone. But he didn't seem to give in, not even to be uncertain. The last few minutes he listened calmly, and obviously he had thought about what to say very carefully.

"That's a really nice story," he said with a note of contempt in his voice. "But I don't really believe that anyone at this table will take this crap seriously. And", his voice turned into a threatening whisper, "I don't want to wrongly suspect any of my colleagues present here, but if this turns out to be a dirty trick with the aim of snatching the boy away and sabotaging my deal, it'll have some serious consequences."

The other men who had looked at him **with hostility** just before, flared up and were furious at this **accusation**. They wouldn't have to do something like that, that would be beneath them, and after all they were respectable businessmen, and so on. For a moment, Justus was afraid that the mood could swing to their disadvantage. If Abelardo were successful in distracting the others from the accusations against him and his club, he might be able to **gain the upper hand** again. If anything, they would then forget about the strange circumstances

---

to eliminate – ausschalten; **with hostility** – feindselig;
accusation – Vorwurf; **to gain the upper hand** –
Oberwasser gewinnen

under which the de la Cruzes arrived at their decision. After all, this was a business deal, and the last thing the clubs' agents wanted, was to make enemies unnecessarily and for no reason. Justus didn't have a choice. Now he had to play his **trump**, hoping that it would be effective. "Uh, Mr. Abelardo," he said, drawing out the words, "it's not necessary to believe us. We can prove it!"

Once again the men fell silent, and Abelardo's face showed no more signs of victory.

"When Pedro was kidnapped he found this rag here on the back seat of the van which he was pushed into, and he took it along with him." Peter gave the First Detective a closed transparent plastic bag with an old blue rag in it. "If you don't mind we'd like to have a police dog **take a whiff at** it. If the dog should be unable to draw a connection between you and the smell of the rag we will immediately apologize for everything and leave at once. But if the opposite should be the case …"

Justus blinked smilingly and shrugged with his shoulders: "the '**testimony**' of a police dog is considered a positive proof in any court."

"Uhuh, a police dog, right?" Abelardo smiled arrogantly. "And you've probably got one with you in your little detective suitcase, don't you?"

"No, not today," Peter replied calmly. "But Inspector Cotta happens to have one out in his car."

With a formal gesture, Peter pointed towards the gray-haired policeman, and Cotta answered with a polite nod. The men at the table were murmuring and looking at the inspector in sur-

---

trump – Trumpf(karte); **to take a whiff at sth.** – an etw. schnuppern; **testimony** – Aussage

prise. Only Abelardo seemed to be more than just surprised. He was visibly shocked at this unexpected **twist** and turned pale as a sheet.

Die drei ??? had called Cotta two days ago and informed him of all the details of the case as well as their plan, and he was more than happy to join them on their trip to San Fernando today. The **collaboration** between him and the three detectives had a long history, even though Cotta wasn't always happy about their activities. But this was something different. The facts were clear, though with quite a complex background story which had taken Cotta a while to fully understand.

"Well, how about it?" Bob looked at Abelardo politely.

The man stared at the tabletop and seemed very **agitated**. "Yes," he said finally with a throaty voice, "yes, alright."

"Well, then I'll go and get Diabolo." Cotta got up, blinked his eyes cheerfully and left the room.

Looking pretty bored, Peter and Bob took their seats again in the background, and Justus put on an uninterested face as well. But deep inside he was far from being calm. Something had to happen now! Right away, because otherwise everything would have been in vain.

"I … I have to go to the bathroom for a minute," Abelardo said at this moment and got up.

'Yes!' Justus was cheering up inwardly, 'go ahead!' Peter and Bob briefly looked up as well but didn't show any reaction. Abelardo moved back his chair and walked around the table – without asking where the bathroom was. And then, all of a

---

twist – (überraschende) Wendung;
collaboration – Zusammenarbeit;
agitated – verstört, unruhig

sudden, he jumped towards the door, tore it open – and ran directly into Cotta's arms who was accompanied by two other officers!
"Well, well, what's the sudden rush?" Cotta grinned at the man with exaggerated friendliness while the two officers grabbed Abelardo's arms on either side. "I think it's time for you to follow us to our headquarters, and then we'll have a little conversation about flowers, knives, numbers, and colors. Isn't that a good idea? What do you think, hmm?"

Master of the deadly slide

"Phew!" Peter stood at the garden gate and watched Cotta leaving with Abelardo. He took a deep sigh of relief. "The bluff with the rag was successful, thank God. The guy was a **tough cookie** all the way to the end."
Justus nodded. "If he hadn't tried to escape it might have been difficult to nail him down. But I don't think that he'll be able to come up with any explanations to prove his **innocence** any longer. And now they will also search his car, his stuff and his hotel room, and hopefully they'll make some interesting discoveries."
Bob grinned. "Perhaps the red armor is still hanging in the **closet**."
"That would be great," Justus laughed. "But I believe that Cotta knows how to get the guy to speak up."
"There was one thing, though, I was wondering about, Just – how did you know that it was actually Abelardo himself who had kidnapped Pedro?" Peter asked. "Because, if Pedro had have been kidnapped in someone else's car, Abelardo wouldn't have cared less about that rag."
"Sad whining songs!" Justus replied mysteriously.
"What?"
"Sad whining songs! Remember, Pedro said the kidnapper had listened to sad whining songs in the car. And that is a very

---

deadly slide – Blutgrätsche; **tough cookie** – harte Nuss, zäher Bursche; **innocence** – Unschuld;
closet – Schrank

accurate description for the melancholic Portuguese **Fado** music. So it was obvious that the man who kidnapped Pedro was Portuguese."

Peter looked at his friend. "Sometimes, Just, I'm really a little scared of you, you know that?"

But before the First Detective was able to reply they heard a slight cough behind them, and die drei ??? turned around. Suddenly all members of the de la Cruz family stood in front of them. They hadn't heard their friends coming closer. While the boys were smiling at them cheerfully, Esperanza smiled a little uncertainly, and Pancho looked at the ground, embarrassed.

"Uhem, listen." Pancho still didn't look at them.

"Yes?"

"Uh, we … we – well, I …," the old man was **hemming and hawing**, "I think we have to apologize … ," he stuttered. "It wasn't correct, the way we … we behaved towards you. I … I hadn't trusted you all this time, whereas all you tried to do was to help us. That's why I, well we wanted to …"

"… apologize," Esperanza completed the sentence.

Almost at once, the three detectives waved it aside. "No, no, you don't have to," Justus replied. "It was really hard to see through Abelardo's dirty tricks. And in the light of your painful past, we can understand very well that you associated the events with your dead son and the story about Antonio de Mendoza. After all, it's what we did at first, too – until I came across the details of the European soccer clubs in the stadium magazine."

"Actually *we* have to apologize," Bob added.

"You?" Pancho looked at the boys for the first time.

"Yes, because you were the only ones we hadn't let in on our

Fado – melancholischer portugiesischer Musik- und Gesangsstil;
to hem and haw – herumdrucksen

plans this afternoon. But after we learned that the agents of the clubs would come to your place today to find out about your decision, we wanted to wait before we informed you about Abelardo's dirty game. Your decision was proof enough that his plan would have worked out."

"Yes … we understand," Pancho said thoughtfully.

"You did a great job." Esperanza patted Peter on the cheek. "But still: we have behaved like two old donkeys, and you don't need to talk us out of that. And now, all of you come back in, please. I'll prepare some tasty lemonade for us!"

The boys laughed, and finally a cheerful, yet still a little embarrassed, smile showed up on Pancho's face. Then they all walked back into the house.

"Hey Just, tell me," Emiliano walked up to the First Detective. "There's a few things that I still don't quite get. For example, the hooting owl and the clock? How did Abelardo do this?"

"I guess with high-quality loudspeakers," Bob answered instead of Justus. "Nowadays there are speakers not much bigger than a cigarette box – in other words, perfect for hiding – which still have a fantastic sound."

"Hmm." Emiliano nodded. "And there's something else I don't get. Why did this Abelardo guy want me to lose the first game with lousy playing? What did he have in mind with that?"

"In my view, he tried to achieve two things," Justus replied this time. "On the one hand, he tried to **put everyone off the scent**, because then we had to consider that perhaps it wasn't not only about Antonio and his revenge but much rather about someone who simply wanted to sabotage the final. And then your poor playing could have had the additional effect of some

---

to put so. off the scent – jmd. auf die falsche Fährte locken

clubs losing their interest in you, because obviously you're not that good, after all."
Emiliano nodded. "Of course! The way I was staggering across the field down there, this would have been only logical."
"Speaking of other clubs," Peter added. "What's the club of your choice now, Emiliano? Inside, there are still quite a few **tempting** offers waiting for you."
They had already reached the veranda, and Emiliano was just about to say something in response, when they suddenly heard a car honking from the street. The boys stopped, turned around and saw a **trim**, middle-aged man get out, open the garden gate, and walk up to them with **resilient** steps.
"Is that another one of these club sharks?" Bob whispered.
"No idea," Emiliano said, "I don't know him, and as far as I know, there was no other agent scheduled for today."
Now the man was at the veranda, took the three steps and stretched out his hand towards Emiliano. "Hello!" he said cheerfully and brushed a strand of hair out of his face. "You are Emiliano de la Cruz, right?" He also briefly looked at and nodded to die drei ??? but he stayed focused on Emiliano.
"Y… yes, and you are?"
"Gregg Martin, I am …"
"… the coach of the US-American U18 National Soccer Team!" Emiliano completed the sentence, completely stunned. "Now I recognize you!"
Peter also knew at once who the man was and looked at him with wide-open eyes.

---

to tempt – verführen, verlocken;
trim – fit, in guter körperlicher Verfassung
resilient – federnd, elastisch

"Yes, exactly." Martin smiled. "Glad to find you here. I … uhh …," he hesitated for a second, "… I saw you at the cup final the day before yesterday. And to be honest, we have been keeping an eye on you for quite some time already."

"Really?" Emiliano grinned, slightly embarrassed.

"Yes, and I came to ask you if you would like to join us – of course only if you don't have any other **commitments** by now – and play for the American U18 National Team."

At first, Emiliano didn't say anything but just stared at Martin in disbelief. The three detectives were stunned and speechless as well. Only Bob whispered "amazing!"

"There's just one thing," Martin added. "If you joined us you would have to stay in the States and not go to Europe, because otherwise it would be impossible to coordinate the team practices."

Gradually, Emiliano's face brightened. And then, after thinking it over briefly, he slowly started to nod. "I … I think," he said, slightly hesitating but fully convinced, "that this is exactly what I wanted. Yes, I would like to play for you! Yes!" he yelled loudly and stretched out his arms. "Yes! Yes! Yes!"

Martin laughed loudly, and die drei ??? heartily congratulated Emiliano, patting him on the back.

This was quite something! Emiliano, El Torbellino, had just become a member of the American U18 National Soccer Team!

But suddenly Martin frowned. "And you …," he said and turned towards Peter, "… aren't you this master of the deadly slide who fouled Emiliano so harshly in the penalty area just before the game was over?"

---

commitment – Verpflichtung

Embarrassed, Peter looked down. "Ahem, yes," he started, "that must be me."
Martin laid one hand on his shoulder. "You know, that was pretty stupid, but otherwise you played a great game. What was your name once more?"
"Peter, Peter Shaw." Slowly, Peter looked up again.
"Well, Peter Shaw," Martin said with a friendly twinkle in his eye, "I guess in the future we'll keep a close eye on you, too!"
For a second, they were all speechless. Then Justus, Bob and Emiliano jumped onto Peter and, laughing and cheering, the boys **strutted** back into the house.

---

to strut – (hier:) stolzieren

Leseprobe

Die drei ??? – Poisoned E-Mail
erzählt von Ben Nevis

Aus dem Deutschen ins
amerikanische Englisch
übertragen von Andreas Zantop

[...] Another call was coming in, and the answering machine switched on. "For sure it's Aunt Mathilda; I guess she found the note and now she wants to tell me she's sorry," Justus guessed. But then a female voice, unknown to him, sounded through the speaker.

The woman seemed a little **insecure**. "Hello … this is Meg Baker. I need help. It's about … **jellyfish**, yes, these awful creatures in the ocean; they have attacked me by e-mail! How can I describe it? Oh, I hate talking to answering machines! The jellyfish was hidden in an e-mail addressed to me … and now the poison is in my computer! It's shocking! You can't imagine this … You are detectives, aren't you? I've got your phone number from a friend of mine that you had helped out once before. I urgently have to talk to you. I expect you to call me back soon!" She left a telephone number on the machine. Then the tape stopped.

---

insecure – unsicher, verunsichert; **jellyfish** – Qualle(n)

Justus looked at the display. "She called two hours ago," he said. "We shouldn't waste any time and call her back immediately."
"Call back whom?" The door suddenly opened and Bob stepped in. He had caught Justus's last words. But actually it didn't really interest him. Under his left arm he carried a bike tire. His face spoke volumes. "When I turned the corner I hit a nail. Flat. Fortunately, it's only the front tire. You guys could have waited for me, really!"
Bob looked so angry that Justus had to laugh. "We'll take care of your bike later. Looks like we've got a new case. One Mrs. Baker left a message on the answering system and said something about jellyfish poison in her computer."
The third detective stared at him as if Justus had just announced the arrival of **extraterrestrials**. "Jellyfish poison in the computer? These blubbery transparent creatures I'm always afraid of when swimming in the ocean? Seems to me, the lady has confused her computer for her aquarium."
"How funny," Justus answered. "She sounded more like she felt threatened."
"It does sound really strange," Peter remarked. "Probably a computer virus. I guess she caught it per e-mail and now it's wreaking **havoc** in her computer. In that case, she would need the help of a computer expert rather than ours."
"Someone like Tom." Justus picked on his lower lip. Tom was a classmate who was rather silent but otherwise quite okay. Outside of school he seemed to be busy on his computer all the time. From time to time he sent Justus strange mails that obviously were supposed to be funny. Actually he was sending more mails than he was talking.

---

extraterrestrials – Außerirdische; **havoc** – Chaos, Verwüstung

"Didn't Tom once own an aquarium?" Bob asked.
"That's right! Back when he was still putting up with live fish. Meanwhile, he's got them all virtual in his computer. This way, he doesn't have to feed them any longer."
"Justus," Peter **admonished** him, "you always come up with these foreign words! Instead of 'virtual' one can also say 'seeming'."
"You sound almost like those **sulky** members of the Society for the **Purification** of Language! I prefer to express myself in precise terms, after all!"
Bob thought it was about time to change subjects, before an argument would start. "Now go ahead, call back this Mrs. Baker!", he suggested, really **determined**. "Then we'll find out what this jellyfish thing is all about."

Möchtest du wissen, wie dieses Abenteuer für Justus, Peter und Bob ausgeht? Dann frage in deiner Buchhandlung nach:
Die drei ??? – Poisoned E-Mail
ISBN 978-3-440-10065-3

---

to admonish – (er)mahnen, rügen; **sulky** – angesäuert, mürrisch; **purification** – Reinigung; **determined** – entschlossen, entschieden

Die drei ???®

Genauso spannend:

- ☐ **Angriff der Computerviren** 978-3-440-10342-5
- ☐ **Fußball-Gangster** 978-3-440-10343-2
- ☐ **Vampir im Internet** 978-3-440-10344-9
- ☐ **und das Geisterschiff** 978-3-440-10345-6
- ☐ **Todesflug** 978-3-440-10346-3
- ☐ **Labyrinth der Götter** 978-3-440-10347-0
- ☐ **Botschaft von Geisterhand** 978-3-440-10348-7
- ☐ **Insektenstachel** 978-3-440-10350-0
- ☐ **Tal des Schreckens** 978-3-440-10349-4
- ☐ **Hexenhandy** 978-3-440-10352-4
- ☐ **Doppelte Täuschung** 978-3-440-10351-7
- ☐ **Gift per E-Mail** 978-3-440-10353-1
- ☐ **Das Erbe des Meisterdiebs** 978-3-440-10354-8
- ☐ **und der Nebelberg** 978-3-440-10355-5
- ☐ **und der Schatz der Mönche** 978-3-440-10356-2
- ☐ **Die sieben Tore** 978-3-440-10357-9
- ☐ **Panik im Park** 978-3-440-10358-6
- ☐ **Höhle des Grauens** 978-3-440-10359-3
- ☐ **Gefährliches Quiz** 978-3-440-10360-9
- ☐ **Der Feuerteufel** 978-3-440-10363-0
- ☐ **Das Auge des Drachen** 978-3-440-10361-6
- ☐ **Schlucht der Dämonen** 978-3-440-10362-3
- ☐ **Villa der Toten** 978-3-440-10364-7
- ☐ **Auf tödlichem Kurs** 978-3-440-10367-8
- ☐ **Codename: Cobra** 978-3-440-10366-1
- ☐ **Der finstere Rivale** 978-3-440-10365-4
- ☐ **Das düstere Vermächtnis** 978-3-440-10369-2
- ☐ **Der schwarze Skorpion** 978-3-440-10370-8
- ☐ **Der geheime Schlüssel** 978-3-440-10368-5
- ☐ **und der Geisterzug** 978-3-440-10208-4
- ☐ **Spur ins Nichts** 978-3-440-10209-1
- ☐ **Fußballfieber** 978-3-440-10207-7
- ☐ **Schrecken aus dem Moor** 978-3-440-10203-9
- ☐ **Feuermond Teil 1–3** Drei Bände €/D 14,90 978-3-440-10205-3
- ☐ **Geister-Canyon** 978-3-440-10204-6
- ☐ **SMS aus dem Grab** 978-3-440-10515-3
- ☐ **Schatten über Hollywood** 978-3-440-10577-1
- ☐ **Schwarze Madonna** 978-3-440-10443-9

Auf Englisch:

- ☐ **The Curse of the Cell Phone** 978-3-440-10064-6
- ☐ **Poisoned E-Mail** 978-3-440-10065-3
- ☐ **Soccer Mania** 978-3-440-10640-2

Jeder Band mit 128 Seiten, ab 10 Jahren
Je € 7,90; €/A 8,20; sFr 14,10
Preisänderungen vorbehalten

www.kosmos.de

KOSMOS